Diablo – The Bequest

Gabi Adam

Diablo – The Bequest

Copyright: © 2006 Gabi Adam
The plot and the names of the characters are entirely fictional.
Original title: Das Vermächtnis
Published by PONY, Stabenfeldt A/S
Cover photo: Bob Langrish
Cover layout: Stabenfeldt A/S
Translated by Barclay House Publishing
Typeset by Roberta L. Melzl
Edited by Marie Javins
Printed in Germany 2005

ISBN: 1-933343-14-1

Stabenfeldt, Inc.
457 North Main Street
Danbury, CT 06811
www.pony.us

For Fengor, my first great horse-love.

Chapter 1

Ricki Sulai woke up earlier than usual. The anticipation of meeting her friends Cathy Sutherland and Lillian Bates, and her boyfriend Kevin Thomas, for their previously arranged riding date had made it impossible for her to lie in bed. And besides, there was work to do.

She dressed quickly and hurried to the stable, where she groomed and brushed her black gelding, Diablo, to a high sheen. Glancing at her wristwatch, the thirteen-year-old saw that she still had forty-five minutes before her friends were supposed to show up. They always assembled at Ricki's house because in addition to Diablo, the Sulais' stable also housed Lillian's Doc Holliday, Kevin's Sharazan, Cathy's foster horse Rashid, and even the Bates' family donkey, Chico.

Ricki returned to her room and plopped down on her bed. She closed her eyes contentedly, crossed her arms behind her head, and began to daydream.

Life is great, she thought. *Thanks to Jake, I have Diablo to ride and care for, and Cathy, Lillian, and Kevin are three of the best friends anyone could wish for.*

It was true. The four teenagers were a very close-knit group, made even closer by the adventures (Brigitte, Ricki's mother, called them "scrapes") they had shared over the past few months. Sometimes, however, the quartet became a quintet. Lillian's boyfriend, Josh, a fan of the western saddle, often joined them on their riding excursions with his little spotted mare, Cherish. He was full of fun and always clowned around. "Josh never runs out of ways to make us laugh," Lillian often claimed.

Kevin had a different opinion: "The best part about Josh is that his father owns the riding shop so we all get discounts," he would reply, a trace of envy in his voice.

It's too bad that Cathy doesn't have a boyfriend; then we'd be an even half-dozen, Ricki was thinking when she heard the familiar sound of a bike bell outside her window.

"Hey, Ricki, are you up there? Are you sleeping?" Kevin's loud voice shattered her reverie. She jumped off the bed and flew to the window.

"Kevin! Don't make so much noise. I'm coming!" she called down to him. Then she turned and ran out of her bedroom. She sprang down the stairs, and two minutes later was standing in front of her boyfriend, who beamed at her.

"What's up, Ricki? Are the horses already brushed and saddled?" Kevin asked impatiently.

"Men!" Ricki huffed in mock exasperation. Then she stuck her tongue out at him, taking his arm at the same time.

"Are the others here yet?" the boy asked.

"Nope, but I'm sure they'll show up pretty soon. Lillian told me that we'll hook up with Josh later. She also said that she's got a big surprise for us. I can't wait to find out

6

what it is," exclaimed Ricki as she pushed the stable door wide open.

"Surprises are always fun," agreed Kevin. He had to raise his voice a little to be heard over the loud whinnying of the horses. "It's okay, guys!" Kevin grinned at the excited animals and ran over to his long-legged roan. Ricki – already at Diablo's stall – watched the boy take out a handful of sugar cubes from his jeans pocket and distribute them to the horses. She noticed that Sharazan got a little more than the rest. *He really loves that horse*, she thought, touched by the obvious and special affection Kevin showed his Sharazan.

"Hi, Kevin," Jake, the stable hand, called out as he walked through the door of the stable.

"Hey, Jake! What's up? Everything okay?"

The old man squinted his eyes and focused on the roan.

"You shouldn't give him so many sugar cubes. They aren't good for horses!" he grumbled instead of answering.

"Oh, Jake, normally I give him something else! But I'm broke right now so I can't buy him any herbal treats." Kevin tried weakly to defend himself.

"They would be much healthier!"

"I know, but do you have any idea how expensive they are?" groaned Kevin.

Jake wouldn't let it go. "How much is the health of your horse worth to you?" he asked a little harshly.

Kevin knew he was about to get a scolding from Jake, so he was relieved to see Cathy and Lillian come running in. Now he wouldn't have to come up with another lame excuse. He'd never be able to convince Jake that Sharazan's good health meant everything to him. Jake was right – no question – but that wasn't going to stop Kevin from slipping Sharazan a "sweet treat" from time to time.

"Hey, Jake, how're ya doing?" called Lillian. Cathy chimed in, "Hiya, Jake, how's everything?"

The old man shook his head and started to walk toward the door on his way outside.

"I must look pretty bad if everyone has to ask me how I'm doing! I'm beginning to think …"

"Oh, Jake, we were just trying to be nice, but now that I'm getting a good look at you, you look great, full of vitality, action, full of –" Cathy chattered on, but Jake waved her aside brusquely.

"Oh, leave me be!" he pleaded. "You don't mean all those things anyway! And besides, I've already looked at myself in the mirror this morning!"

"And? Didn't you see a beaming young man? After all, you're only as old as you feel, right?" Cathy teased.

Jake shook his finger at her and then left the stable.

Those kids, he thought, smiling. *Impudent, but they always make me laugh. And, for all their impudence, I know they care. Good kids.*

"Thanks, guys. You showed up just in time." Kevin breathed a sigh of relief. "Jake was about to lecture me on the dangers of giving sugar cubes to horses and –"

"Kevin, don't make such a big deal out of it!" Ricki cut him off. "We all know the only thing that matters to Jake is the health and well-being of the horses. I'd much rather find out what Lillian's surprise is." Ricki stood on her tiptoes and looked over the top of the stall at Lillian, who was cleaning one of her white horse's front hooves.

"Hey, Holli, stop fidgeting! I just want to see if ... oh, good, then I'll do it afterward! I have to go get a hoof pick anyway!"

"Is there something wrong with Holli?" asked Cathy, who was grooming Rashid.

"He got a stupid stone in his hoof yesterday and there was a mark there. It looked like a bruise," replied Lillian. She smoothed her hair back from her face.

"That's too bad. Is he limping?" Ricki held the stall door open for her friend.

"I have no idea. I'll have to see first. If necessary, you guys will have to go riding without me." Lillian ran over to the tack room to get a hoof pick and then she carefully led her horse out onto the yard.

"Did you guys notice anything?"

Ricki and Kevin both shook their heads. "Nope! He's not limping! Everything's all right," Ricki said, trying to reassure her friend.

"Okay, then," said Lillian, relieved. She came back into the stable. "Maybe we can ride a softer trail today ..."

"Of course!" Ricki nodded. She began to saddle Diablo.

"Hey, slow down! I still have to groom Sharazan!" yelled Kevin.

"We always have to wait for the guys." Cathy grinned and kissed Rashid on his muzzle. The dun-colored horse looked at her with huge eyes and then shook his beautiful head. He snorted.

"You must have bad breath!" Kevin shot back in retaliation.

"Tell me, Ricki, how can you stand this guy?" asked Lillian.

Ricki shrugged her shoulders and gave a long-suffering look. "I ask myself the same question sometimes! But anyway, Lily, what about the surprise you promised? Are we going to find out what it's about sometime today?"

"Wouldn't you like to know, but guess what? Because I've told you how I hate to be called Lily, I'm going to keep you in suspense a little longer. Let's go riding first!"

"Aw, bummer! And I thought you were my friend!" Ricki made a face, showing her displeasure. But then suddenly she laughed. "I know what it is!" she claimed, rubbing her hands together.

"Oh, really? Then tell us!" Lillian grinned.

"You baked something!" guessed Ricki.

"That's great! What did you make?" interrupted Kevin, who was a total pastry freak.

Lillian couldn't stop laughing. "Well, it depends on how you look at it," she said, without giving anything else away. Instead, she led her Doc Holliday outside.

"Can we leave?" Lillian asked. She tightened the saddle girth before mounting.

"Of course!" "Sure!" "Let's go!" they all answered at once, and then the four friends rode their horses away from the farm.

Chico hee-hawed, a little insulted at being left behind – again. He could never understand why he wasn't allowed to accompany his horse friends on their excursions. His only comfort was that Ricki's little brother, Harry, usually spent a lot of time with him then so that he didn't get bored. He stretched his neck upward in order to get a look over the wall of his stall to see if the boy was around. Surely Harry would show up soon.

*

"Hey, where are we anyway? We've never been here before. I thought I knew all the trails around Echo Lake like the back of my hand!" Cathy stopped Rashid and looked around, astonished.

Lillian grinned. "You're right! I've only known about this trail since yesterday. Josh showed it to me."

"Right, that's how it happened!" The three shouted at once, and then Ricki, Kevin, and Cathy laughed so loud that their horses started twitching their ears back and forth.

"What's that supposed to mean?" asked Lillian, annoyed. "Idiots!" she declared, which made all three of them laugh even louder.

"All right, what's going on? Do you just want to keep fooling around, or – Okay, if you're not interested in my surprise, then –"

"Quiet!" Ricki quit laughing on the spot. "Hey, it's about Lillian's surprise! Did you hear?"

"Of course! Did you hide your cake in the woods?" giggled Cathy, as she wiped the tears from her eyes.

Lillian rolled her eyes with exasperation. "Are you guys coming or do you plan on turning around and riding back home? She was just about to turn her horse when her friends gestured for her to stop.

"No, no! We're coming!"

"Great! Let's go."

The four of them rode single file, along the trail through the woods. The path became narrower and narrower.

"We're almost there," shouted Lillian.

11

"Where is there?" asked Ricki.

"You'll see in a few minutes!"

"You've been saying that for at least half an hour," complained Cathy, who was at least as anxious as Ricki to know what the surprise was. Kevin was the only one who didn't seem concerned.

"I don't care where Lillian serves her cake," he said, and let Sharazan amble on with a loose rein.

"Hey, do you guys hear that?" Ricki stopped suddenly and listened intensely.

"What? Oh yeah. Sounds like music, doesn't it?" Cathy looked puzzled.

"Music? Who could possibly be making music out here?" asked Kevin, but then a few moments later he also heard the sounds of a guitar.

"Ta-dah!" heralded Holli's rider as she guided her horse into a beautiful clearing right after the last curve in the trail.

Amazed, Lillian's friends stopped their horses and stared at what they saw in front of them.

It was an old hunting cabin, and someone had built a campfire – in a safe space lined with stones – for a barbecue.

Around the fire were about forty sitting or standing young people, all dressed in jeans and boots. They were wearing cowboy hats and elaborate leather vests, the "uniform" of riders who favor western riding. They'd driven poles into the ground around the clearing, with rings to tie up their horses that were standing around quietly, one next to the other.

Josh sat on the wooden steps that led up to the cabin. He was playing a cowboy ballad on his guitar.

"Amazing!" was the only thing that Cathy could say.

12

"A cowboy party in the middle of the woods! Wow, Lillian, that's cool! This is a *real* surprise." Ricki smiled with delight.

"I didn't know Josh could play the guitar," said Kevin, genuinely impressed. He loved country music, and anyone who could play guitar went up a notch or two in his eyes. He had never managed to get the instrument to sound good, despite trying several times to teach himself to play. Somehow the strings seemed not to want him to play them. They'd given off a harsh and unpleasant sound, so Kevin had quit trying to learn to play the guitar.

Josh put down his guitar immediately and walked over to his friends.

"Hey, I'm really glad you came! Lily …" He helped the girl out of the saddle gallantly and gave her a huge hug. "I missed you very much," he whispered quietly and kissed her on the forehead.

"I missed you, too," breathed Lillian, gazing at him lovingly. "Have you been here long?"

"Hmm, about an hour and a half, I think. But you guys got here just at the right time. You haven't missed anything!"

"Y'know, Josh, your girlfriend can really keep a secret. She never told us anything about this place. It's really cool here!" Kevin jumped down from Sharazan's back directly in front of Josh.

"Have you ever seen so many checkered horses all in one place?" Cathy couldn't stop shaking her head.

"They're called piebalds," explained Josh.

"Are they all from around here? I never knew there were so many Western-style riders in the area," Ricki joined in.

13

"We're a real club," explained Josh with pride. "These folks are really nice people – and they have great horses – but you'll see that later. Just sit back and let yourselves be surprised."

"C'mon," he added. "You can tie up your horses over there."

"But we didn't bring any halters with us," Ricki realized.

Lillian, a satisfied look on her face, pulled four narrow halters out of her jacket pockets. "You can't say that I didn't think of everything," she grinned.

"Sponsored by Josh's father, I presume," Kevin laughed and took one of the halters for Sharazan.

"Of course! It only cost me a few bats of my eyelashes," exclaimed Lillian.

"Come on, you guys," urged Josh. "I want to introduce you to my friends."

The kids quickly exchanged their horses' bridles for the lightweight halters, loosened the saddle girths, and tied their horses to the posts. Josh had several ropes ready and was impatiently shuffling back and forth from one leg to the other.

"Hey, Josh, what's up? When are you going to play again?" a high voice shouted from a distance, but Josh just ignored it. He wanted to pay attention to Lillian and her friends for a while.

"I've got to get a closer look at these magnificent horses," said Ricki. "Cathy's right. You don't often see so many piebald horses at once. Josh, where are they usually?"

"Some stay at the stable where I board Cherish, but they stay in other nearby towns as well. Actually, my club friends

14

don't live around here. That's why you probably only know a few of them." Josh took Lillian's hand and they ran over to the circle of young people together.

"Hey, everyone," shouted Josh, beaming. "I'd like to introduce my girlfriend, Lillian. And this is Ricki, Cathy, and Kevin. They're not Western-style riders, but they're still all right!" he added.

"Well, that was a really sweet introduction," grinned Cathy as she poked Ricki, who was drawn magically to a beautiful black-and-white piebald gelding.

"Wow, that horse over there is fabulous," she began to gush. "I think I have to go –" And she disappeared.

"She isn't going to abandon Diablo, is she?" asked Kevin, but Lillian just tapped her forehead.

"It would be more likely for the sun not to come up," she replied as she focused again on Josh, who had observed Ricki walking away with a shrug of his shoulders.

"That's typical of Ricki: The horses come first. So, now pay attention." Josh pointed from one Western-style rider to another as he ran through their names.

There were Kim and Andre, both dressed alike; Marty, who had a Stetson with an amazing hatband featuring Navajo embroidery and turquoise stones; and Sandra and Michelle, who looked "totally awesome," as Cathy said a little enviously, with their leather vests covered in fringe.

"And over there are Pepe, Gringo, and Jenny," Josh continued.

"Josh, that's too many names to remember. I think it'll be easier to find out in a conversation what their names are," Lillian laughed.

"To be honest, the only thing I caught is that the black-haired one in the leather vest isn't Pepe," admitted Kevin. He turned back toward Ricki to see where she had gone. Was she still admiring that checkered horse?

The girl was standing next to the horse and speaking softly to him while stroking his neck.

"You are really beautiful," she murmured. "How is it possible that I have never seen you before? I'm sure that I would have noticed you. Oh well, sometimes I just walk around blindly. Tell me, what kind of a horse are you? I don't know much about Western-style horses, but you don't care about that, do you? Do you want a treat? Diablo won't see us." Ricki searched around in her jeans pocket for an herbal pellet, which the animal was delighted to accept.

"Do you always do that?" A male voice made Ricki jump. Nervously, she turned around and found herself staring into an attractive smiling face.

"What do you mean?" she asked awkwardly. She felt herself turning red.

"You give treats to strange horses. Some owners don't like that!"

"Oh. Is this your horse?"

The young man nodded.

"And are you one of those owners who –"

"Nope! Charon really likes treats, so I'm happy when other people give them to him. By the way, my name is Alex, but most people call me Lex. Why all the formality? I'm not that old. I'm nineteen."

"You look much older! I'm Ricki."

Lex laughed loudly. "At least you're honest! Good thing

I'm not a girl, otherwise I'd probably be mad that you thought I looked older!"

"Your horse is – I don't know how to describe it – he's just incredible!" Ricki turned her attention back to Charon. He was curious and blew air into her face.

"Hmm, he seems to like you. It's not often that he likes someone right away," responded Lex. He observed Ricki at least as closely as his horse did.

"Are you a new member in the western club? I've never seen you at our events."

"Oh no, I haven't been to any. I'm here with my friends, because Josh –" began Ricki, but she was interrupted right away by Lex.

"Oh, you're the ones! Joe has told us a lot about you!" he said.

"Well, I hope it was all good!" Ricki had to laugh to herself. *Joe?* She wondered if Lillian knew what this club called her boyfriend.

Kevin watched Ricki out of the corners of his eyes. He couldn't pay attention to Josh and he had a funny feeling in his stomach. What kind of guy was she talking to for so long? And her eyes were sparkling.

"Hey, Josh, who's that over there?" he heard Cathy ask suddenly.

"Who? The guy with Ricki? That's Lex, one of my best pals! He's really a good guy. By the way, that's his horse that Ricki is admiring!"

"Does he have a girlfriend?" Lillian wanted to know.

Josh looked at her skeptically. "Why would you want to know that? Aren't I good enough for you anymore?"

"Don't be an idiot!" Lillian laughed. "Of course it's not that, but Cathy is still alone –"

Now Josh had to grin as well.

Cathy was tempted to jab Lillian in the ribs, but then she changed her mind.

"That's true, and that Lex! Wow, he's really cute."

Kevin groaned to himself. Cute! That was all he needed! But from the way things looked, Cathy wasn't the only one into Lex! Ricki –

"Come on, let's go join them" announced Josh. He started walking toward them.

"Hey, Lex," he shouted. "Are we bothering you two?"

"Of course! You always interrupt me when I'm talking to attractive young ladies," winked Josh's friend as he put his arm around Ricki's shoulder.

The girl laughed too. She looked at Kevin, who gave her a critical look.

Huh, she thought. *He isn't jealous, is he?*

"Charon has a new girlfriend," said Lex just then as he untied his horse. "Come with me," he said, and then he walked over to a fenced-in square with his arm still around Ricki. The horse followed him like a dog.

"Aren't you afraid Charon will run away?" asked Ricki. She kept looking back over her shoulder, remembering that Diablo had run off more than once.

"He wouldn't do that. He is very well-trained – watch this!"

Lex began to run in zigzags, so that Ricki almost stumbled. But Charon followed his owner step for step, with his head just behind Lex. Suddenly Lex let go of Ricki and stepped directly in front of his horse. "Catch me," he shouted merrily to his horse.

Charon paid close attention to every slight motion that Lex made. With tensed muscles, the animal was ready to head off his owner immediately. If Lex wanted to get by him on the right, Charon jumped in the same direction. When the young man tried to avoid Charon on the left, the horse stayed in front of him. There was no possibility of escape.

Lex and Charon interacted like this for several minutes while Ricki, Cathy, and Lillian watched with amazement.

Kevin was getting angry. What was the big deal about this childish trick? And look how Ricki was gazing at Lex with awe –

"I'm beginning to wonder why we even came here," he mumbled grumpily to himself, as his original good mood began to disappear.

"That's called 'cutting,'" Lex explained to the girls. He was completely out of breath. "On ranches out west, working horses are trained to separate out single cows from a herd. They cut them off from escaping when the cows have to be branded. So in this case, I'm the cow, and Charon isn't going to let me get by him!" laughed Lex. Completely exhausted, he leaned against his horse.

You really are a cow, Kevin thought nastily, before going over to Ricki.

"Wanna go over and look after the horses?" he asked his girlfriend while reaching for her hand. But Ricki just shook him off.

"We just tied them up," she responded while continuing to stroke Charon's forehead. "Is it difficult to ride western?"

"No more difficult than English," he answered. Before Ricki realized what was happening, he had pushed her beside Charon. "Just try it. Like I said, he's really well trained and he does almost everything by himself! I'll tell you what to do, then nothing can go wrong."

Without another thought, Ricki mounted the horse. Of course, the stirrups were too long, but that didn't matter, because the girl sat in the saddle very securely.

"Let the reins hang loose. Charon, go!" Lex ran ahead, and the horse followed him without Ricki having to do anything.

"Wow, Lex, may I ride him, too?" called Cathy, her eyes shining.

"Of course!"

"Great!" The girl was delighted. While she watched Ricki and Charon, she realized that her gaze kept returning to Lex, and that actually she was more interested in being near him than in doing any Western-style training.

I think I've got a crush on him, Cathy realized suddenly. She looked at Lillian, Josh, and Kevin, but they were all watching Charon. Well, at least Lillian and Josh were. Kevin was looking more and more sullen, and then, mumbling something incomprehensible, he turned around and went back to Sharazan.

"Hey, you're doing really well." Kevin heard Lex praising Ricki and Ricki's answering laugh.

"He's really coming on to her!" Kevin ground his teeth. In that moment, he sensed that something had changed in his relationship with Ricki. And he didn't like it at all.

Chapter 2

"You're a natural!" exclaimed Lex, as Ricki dismounted after a half hour of riding Charon., Her heart was beating wildly.

"No, I'm not, but this horse is a genius," she said breathlessly. Ricki had always thought that no other horse would react as well to her instructions as Diablo, but Charon ... all she had to do was *think* about what she was planning to do next, and while she changed her position in the saddle the horse did exactly what he had been trained to do. Of course, he had listened to the voice of his owner and he knew all of his commands by heart, but nevertheless, Charon was incredible!

"Do you think Diablo could be trained like this?" asked Ricki hopefully.

"I don't know." Lex's expression was undecided. "In principle, you can train any horse to do this, but how well he does it depends somewhat on his breeding. You know, if the animal is too big or too heavy, or if it doesn't have enough energy, then it can be a little difficult. I'd have to look at your Diablo."

"Right now?" Ricki wanted to know.

"Of course, why not?" Lex took hold of Charon's reins in his right hand and Ricki's hand with his left. He led Charon back to where he had been tied up. Apparently he'd completely forgotten that he'd promised to let Cathy ride his horse.

Baffled, Cathy watched the two walk away. A feeling of disappointment was growing inside of her. Or maybe it was jealousy. Ricki seemed to have won Lex's heart.

Ricki walked easily beside the young man and laughed happily when one of his friends called over to them: "Hey, Lex, you have a new girlfriend? Where did you find her?"

"Charon picked her out for me! He has good taste, don't you think?"

"Perfect! The only thing missing is the outfit! Girl, come over here!" Peter Snyder, alias Gringo, waved to her. Ricki looked puzzled but nonetheless went toward him.

"Here, you can borrow my Stetson! Pepe, do you have another vest in the car?"

"Yeah, why?" came the reply.

"We have to outfit Lex's new girlfriend!" said Gringo. Lex laughed loudly and Ricki blushed a little once again.

For a moment, she thought about Kevin. Where was he anyway? She looked around and saw him with Sharazan. He appeared to be in a very bad mood.

Uh-oh, thought Ricki. *What's eating him? All I did was ride Charon.*

"There, young lady, now you really belong!" Pepe helped her put on a short leather vest with fringes and suddenly Ricki felt like a different person.

It can't be just the clothes, she thought, baffled. She thanked the young man.

"Hey, that's great! I'll return the outfit to you before I ride home," she promised.

"That's okay! Have fun!" Pepe said goodbye and then ran toward the cabin.

"Man, that really looks good on you! You should ride Charon again. Your friends would really be jealous then." Lex smiled at her, and Ricki felt her knees go weak. "Well, let's go visit Diablo before we get something to eat. Are you hungry? We have a huge pot of beans simmering, and steak and potatoes are cooking back at the campfire."

Ricki nodded. "Delicious! I can't wait!" Her heart was in her throat as she looked at the young man walking beside her.

*

Kevin was seething with jealousy as he watched Ricki and Lex walking toward him.

"Hey, Kevin, how come you took off so quickly?" Ricki called to him. But the boy gave no answer.

"Charon is fan-tas-tic!" Ricki tried again to get a conversation going, but the only thing Kevin said was, "Diablo ... it looks like we're through!"

Ricki hesitated and looked awkwardly at Lex. He just shrugged his shoulders.

"What's that supposed to mean?" she asked, but Kevin was in no mood to explain anything. "Idiot!" Ricki snarled as she went past him.

Diablo was obviously glad to see the girl. He snorted a greeting and knocked the Stetson off her head.

"Well, at least *you're* not mad at me," said Ricki with a sidelong glance at Kevin. She patted Diablo's shiny neck lovingly.

Lex whistled admiringly when he saw the animal. He walked around the horse slowly, examining him with the eye of an expert.

"Are you a professional animal trainer, or what?" asked Kevin acidly, but Lex didn't let it bother him.

"No, my dad's a veterinarian and I've been helping him for as long as I can remember. I'm in my first year as a pre-vet student," he explained. Then, turning to Ricki, he said, "Ricki, you have a really beautiful horse! He's fairly large, but I think it would be possible to train him. How does he react to signals?"

"Very well!" said Ricki proudly. She found it exciting to have a future veterinarian standing next to her.

"May I ride him?" Lex had gone over to Diablo and was rubbing him between the ears lovingly.

"Of course. Do you want to do it now?"

Lex nodded, and Ricki immediately began to pull the snaffle over her horse's head.

Kevin had stepped back a bit. *A pre-vet student! Well, of course, I don't have a chance against him! But this guy is much too old for Ricki*, he thought. He kicked a stone so furiously that it flew past Diablo, nearly hitting the animal.

"Kevin, are you crazy, or what?" Ricki turned around fast and gave her boyfriend a dirty look. "Would you please tell

24

me what's wrong with you? Ever since we got here, you've been in a bad mood! Why did you come with us in the first place?"

"I didn't know what was going to happen."

"That's the way it is with surprises. You don't know in advance what's going to happen!"

Lex looked back and forth at the two of them. "Do you two need to talk? We can deal with Diablo later."

"No, we don't have anything to talk about!" Ricki was furious. "Come on, Lex, I'm anxious to see how Diablo reacts to you!"

The young man shrugged his shoulders. "Okay!"

Ricki untied her horse and led him over to the designated training area.

On her way she scowled at Kevin and said pointedly, "Aren't you ashamed of yourself for acting this way?"

Kevin had an answer ready but he managed to swallow it.

Ricki tried to put on an innocent expression as she noticed Cathy, who was standing near them with a look of disappointment on her face.

"Guess what! Lex is going to see if Diablo can be trained as a Western-style horse. Cool, isn't it?" she yelled to her, but it was obvious that Cathy didn't share her friend's enthusiasm.

"Yeah, great!" she answered in a flat voice, feeling a little slighted.

Ricki hesitated. "And what's wrong with you? Kevin's already acting weird, and now you're starting to –"

"Forget it!" Cathy cut her off.

"They're all acting crazy today," she murmured quietly to herself as she continued to lead Diablo to the training area.

"Are your friends always like this?" Lex wanted to know.

"Normally, no. Maybe it's the weather," she responded. She tried an uncertain smile.

"Well, since the sun is shining brightly, I'd hate to see how they behave when it rains! So, give me your little black devil. Let's see what he can do."

Lex took Diablo's reins, tightened the girth, and swung into the saddle. For a few minutes, the horse seemed confused – uncertain as to whether he should permit this stranger to ride him – but Lex spoke to Diablo in a voice that was pleasantly low and quiet, which seemed to calm him down. Soon he was reacting to Lex's leg signals and trotted well around the training area.

After a while the young man let the reins fall loose, and he held them farther apart as he changed his position to be a little more forward. While the horse was just walking, Lex began to get him accustomed to the Western style of riding by using exaggerated signals, just as they did with other young Western horses in training. And soon the black horse understood what Lex wanted him to do.

"Hey, he's really good," Lex said when he jumped down from the saddle after half an hour. "In spite of his size, he's very agile, and he's a quick learner."

Ricki's heart swelled with pride, especially after several of the other Western riders gave her the thumbs-up signal.

"Young lady, would you like to join our club?" Pepe shouted over to Ricki. Josh, who had just arrived with Lillian, was immediately in agreement.

"I think that's a great idea!" he nodded, beaming. "I'd

26

be even happier if I could get you to join our club," he whispered to Lillian.

"No, no. My dear old Holli wouldn't be able to do it," said Lillian, laughing. "By the way, where are Cathy and Kevin?"

"No idea. For some unknown reason, both of them are mad!" was Ricki's response, as she stepped outside the training area with Lex and Diablo.

"They're in a bad mood? That's not possible! We're well-known for always being in a good mood!" Josh gave his girlfriend a kiss. "I'll go and see if I can find them."

*

"Josh doesn't need to look for them," said Ricki somewhat sadly to Lex as they went to tie up Diablo. On the pole where Rashid and Sharazan had been tied, only the halters were hanging limply from the ropes. Cathy and Kevin had obviously ridden back home.

"Hmm," said Lex. "Is Kevin your boyfriend?"

Ricki nodded. "Yeah, but ..." She began to stutter a little. At the moment she wasn't so sure how she felt about him. Lex seemed so much more like her. His whole manner was completely different from Kevin's. That couldn't be due to the fact that he was a few years older, could it?

"Well, come on, don't worry about it," said Lex. "It'll be all right."

Ricki shrugged her shoulders. "I don't know. I think Kevin might be jealous!"

27

At a loss for words, Lex stared at her and began to laugh out loud. "Jealous? Of whom? Not of me, I hope!"

Ricki turned bright red and lowered her eyes. In that instant, Lex realized how serious the situation was.

He immediately stopped laughing. "Girl ... don't tell me he has reason to be," he said softly. He put his hand under her chin and lifted up her face.

"Maybe," Ricki admitted shyly. Then she tore herself away, threw the reins over Diablo's head, and jumped into the saddle without using the stirrups. "See you," she said to the perplexed Lex. She turned her horse and galloped off as though the devil were after her.

"What the –?" mumbled Lex, while he stared after her, completely baffled.

"Hey, did you tell Ricki one of your stupid jokes? Why did she gallop away as though she'd just been stung by a bee?" Josh wanted to know.

Lex shook his head. "No, Josh. I seem to have a little problem here. I think Ricki has developed a crush on me!"

"Are you serious?" asked Josh, sure that Lex was joking with him, as he always did.

"Absolutely serious! It looks as though Kevin got jealous and took off. I don't know what Cathy had to do with all this. I haven't figured that out yet!" exclaimed Lex.

Josh couldn't keep himself from grinning. "Ah, Lex ... I think you really do have a problem, because Cathy has a thing for you, too. She thinks you're really cute!"

Lex groaned and leaned on Josh's shoulder. "Old buddy, I think only a plate of beans and a rare steak can help me bear all of this flirting!"

"Yeah, so let's go and get some food before the barrel-racing contest starts," suggested Josh.

The two young men went back to the others, where Lillian was waiting for them.

"Didn't find them?" she asked Josh.

He nodded. "I think you're going to have to be satisfied with just me for the rest of the day. Ricki and company have all left!"

"What? Is this a joke?" Lillian looked back and forth at Lex and her boyfriend. She didn't understand what was going on. "You're going to have to explain that to me with a few more details."

*

Ricki had jumped on Diablo and left the clearing so suddenly that she didn't notice that she had taken the wrong trail until they were deep in the woods.

Darn, she thought. She didn't know her way around this area at all. She probably should have ridden back to the group to get directions for getting on the right trail toward home, but she definitely didn't want to do that. She never wanted to see Lex again, she decided. It embarrassed her that she had let him know that she had begun to have feelings for him.

So, she just rode along with Diablo – not too fast – and hoped that they would be out of the woods soon and she would see something that would help her figure out where she was.

Lots of thoughts were racing through her head.

Was it possible that such a thing as "love at first sight" existed? That I saw someone, talked with him, and suddenly knew that I felt more than just friendship for him?

Then Ricki thought about Kevin.

Strange, she had always thought that she was in love with Kevin, but what she had felt toward Lex today – who was quite a bit older – was somehow a completely different feeling, much more intense ... deeper. Oh, how could you describe it?

Nineteen! She began to do some math. *Kevin turned fifteen recently, so that's a four-year age difference! Weird, how much more grown up someone is even when there are only a few years difference in age. But I'm still only thirteen – well, practically fourteen. Oh, why couldn't I be a little older?* she asked herself, and then she began to imagine what it would be like to be together with Lex.

"He's a veterinary student," she told Diablo, who listened attentively. "I want to become a vet, too, and then we could open up a practice together, and –" Suddenly the girl hesitated. "Ricki, quit dreaming! It's all nonsense! You don't even know if Lex likes you!"

But he did let you ride Charon, her inner voice whispered. Confused and upset, Ricki sighed loudly.

"I think being an adult isn't very easy," she said to Diablo, before leaning way down to give him a hug.

If only he could talk, Ricki wished at that moment, as she did so often. Then she sat back up and urged her animal into a trot that soon brought them out of the woods.

"So, my sweetie, let's see where we are," she murmured and looked all around.

They were surrounded mainly by fields and meadows,

but there was also an attractive, renovated farm, which Ricki noticed at once.

"Living around here would appeal to me, too," she announced and decided to ride a little closer. The trail would take her past there anyway.

When she arrived at the back of the building, she saw a small fenced-in paddock. Inside was an adorable little brown pony that hadn't been very well taken care of. Its coat and mane were matted and shaggy.

Immediately, Ricki felt the anger she always felt when she discovered an animal that was obviously being neglected or mistreated by its owners. Outraged, she cut straight across a meadow to get to the paddock more quickly.

"This is unbelievable. These people have a beautifully renovated house but they can't afford to groom their pony. Just look at the poor little thing! It hasn't seen a brush in weeks, that's for sure! What kind of people are capable of neglecting an animal like this?"

Diablo perked up his ears and moved them back and forth. He was listening to what his rider was saying, but his attention was drawn to the little pony, which looked up as it saw the tall black horse moving toward him. It whinnied hesitantly – unsure of itself – and walked stiffly toward the paddock fence before it stopped and stood still.

"They haven't even repaired the fence," Ricki noticed as she moved closer to it.

The wooden poles were rotten and broken off, and the posts leaned dangerously toward the ground. An electric wire that had formerly been stretched between the poles now hung in loose loops around the fence.

Ricki's heart almost stopped beating. *My goodness, that pony is really lucky that he hasn't been caught in that yet*, she thought, as she jumped down from the saddle.

"Hi, little one," she called to the animal softly. "Come here. I won't hurt you." She tried to lure it by stretching out her hand and offering her last treat, but the pony wouldn't budge.

Nervously, it kept laying back its ears. It raised first one foreleg then the other, as though the weight of its body was too much for its legs.

Ricki tried to identify a swelling on its front leg, but that was impossible because she was too far away. In addition, its legs were partially hidden by shrubs and weeds.

"Something is wrong here!" mumbled Ricki. She began thinking of ways to get a better look at the pony. However, she wasn't sure that she was allowed to just slip under the fence and walk onto the paddock. Besides, Diablo was a problem. In order to prevent him from running away, she would have to tie him up, but she didn't have a rope with her, and she couldn't see any poles strong enough to deal with his strength. One tug by him would have been enough to knock down the entire fence.

Ricki stood there undecided for quite a while, as she looked back and forth at the pony and at the farmhouse, which sat so peacefully nearby.

I wonder if anybody's home? she asked herself. Then suddenly she had a horrible thought: Maybe the owner has gone away on a trip and forgotten about the little pony.

The more Ricki thought about it, the more convinced she became that the animal had simply been forgotten.

With a heavy heart, she tore her eyes away from the pony, which had an enormous belly but otherwise seemed nothing but skin and bones. Slowly, Ricki walked toward the house. She pulled Diablo behind her by the reins.

"Come on. At least we have to see if there's anyone here!" she said to her horse, who was snorting and shaking his head.

No one's there! Diablo seemed to be saying, but Ricki kept walking toward the house.

"It looks like someone lives here," she said. She pushed the doorbell, but except for the ding-dong, no sound at all came from within the house.

"That's impossible," murmured Ricki, her finger still on the doorbell.

What will you say if someone opens the door? she suddenly asked herself. She withdrew her hand immediately.

Was it possible just to ring someone's doorbell and say, "Hi, your horse looks neglected"?

"Yes, it was!" decided Ricki. She pulled Diablo a few more yards so that she could look into one of the lower windows.

Inside, everything seemed a little messy, as though the owners had left in a hurry.

Ricki swallowed nervously. She wasn't sure what to do. Then she noticed the mailbox, which was overflowing with mail.

"I knew it! These thoughtless idiots have gone away and left the little pony all on its own! That is such a mean thing to do!"

Disgusted, the girl turned her attention to the mailbox. She pulled everything out at once, hoping to find out who the owners of the little pony were. There was no name anywhere on the door.

She furiously went through all of the mail and finally found something. "Hiram Parker!" she read aloud to Diablo. "Now we know more!" Actually, she still had no idea what to do. However, she knew that she couldn't just leave this pony to fall victim to an uncertain destiny.

Determined, she walked toward the door that led to the connected barn and opened it. She was hoping to find food for the animal. The little patch of edible grass that had grown on the paddock had been eaten down so far that the dirt beneath it was now visible.

"Sorry, Diablo, I can't take you with me in there," she said, as she tied her horse up on the wide hinges of the door with the reins. Just to make sure he couldn't hurt himself, she took out the bit in case he did anything silly.

Then she entered the dusty barn, which smelled damp and moldy, as though no one had been in there for quite some time.

"My goodness, I wonder how long that poor animal has been standing out there?" It must be half-dead from thirst."

In one corner of the stable she found a bucket, and after further searching she finally found a faucet. Unfortunately, her search for food was in vain.

She quickly filled the bucket and dragged it over to the paddock. Without hesitation, she bent down, slipped under the fence, and walked slowly toward the little pony.

"Here. Look what I brought you," she said softly.

A few yards in front of the animal – which she discovered was a mare – she stopped and set the bucket down on the ground. She then calmly walked backward. She knew that the pony would not come over to drink as long as she was nearby.

On her way back, Ricki discovered a tiny stream that seemed to run through the paddock. She breathed a sigh of relief.

"I didn't need to get the bucket," she said to herself quietly. "At least the little mare had something to drink!"

Nevertheless, Ricki decided to leave the bucket there and to go back into the stable. After all, the owners had to have a little hay stored somewhere.

*

Groaning softly, a frail old man lifted his head a few inches – using all his strength – in order to look out of the window. Unhappily, he looked out at his little pony, which had been such a comfort to him since his wife died.

Only four weeks ago, his life had still been in order, until the day he had fallen down in the house after bringing his little Salina to the paddock. Ever since, he was barely able to move. It cost him all his strength just to get to the bathroom and the kitchen, where he fed himself from almost nothing. His supplies were almost used up.

Since he had no more relatives, no one noticed that he could no longer leave the house. And the letter carrier no longer paid any attention, since the time that Parker had shouted at him for teasing Salina through the fence of the paddock.

It was clear to the old man that it was only a matter of time until he was no longer able to carry on without real food. He wouldn't be able to live on canned mushrooms – the only thing he had in great supply – much longer.

Often, his brain didn't seem to be working, and he thought he was a boy again. Sometimes he began calling for his deceased mother or his brother. He was devastated that no one answered.

He had forgotten a long time ago that he had a telephone and – besides the fact that he was hard of hearing and wouldn't have understood anyway – he no longer knew what the thing was used for. That was why he hadn't called for a doctor after his fall.

The only thing he never forgot was Salina, who meant more to him than anything else in the world. His sickness was made worse by the knowledge that he was no longer able to take care of her.

While he held up his head with all his strength and stared outside, he noticed Ricki, who was just leaving the paddock.

"Salina," panted the old man. "Someone is trying to steal Salina, my ... my ... Salina. No, no, NO!" he screamed, fearful that he was going to lose his beloved pony.

Chapter 3

Side by side, Cathy and Kevin rode silently. They hadn't said a word to each other since leaving the clearing. Each was lost in thought; both were disappointed in Ricki and furious at Lex.

"Tell me," Kevin wanted to know, "what does he have that I don't have?"

The girl thought for a long moment and then said, matter-of-factly, "A few years and Charon."

"Is that it?" Kevin laughed bitterly. "Didn't you also say something about him being 'really cute'?"

Cathy blushed. "Yes, I said it," she admitted. "But that was before I found out what a jerk he is. He promises things that he doesn't follow through on, and he's been flirting outrageously with Ricki. Really ..." The girl was obviously hurt.

Kevin looked straight into Cathy's eyes. "What do you mean, 'jerk'!? I bet you have a crush on him, too, and now you're mad at Ricki and jealous of her because she has a better chance with him than you do. Am I right?"

Cathy lowered her eyes. Kevin had hit the nail right on the head, but she was too embarrassed to admit it.

"I don't know who I'm madder at, Ricki or Lex," said Cathy quietly.

Kevin stared straight ahead. After a while, he said in a tense voice, "I am furious at both of them! This Lex character just takes my girlfriend away from me as though it was nothing, brags about being a vet student, and Ricki just falls for his snobby manners! 'He's really well-trained,'" Kevin mocked his new rival, "'He does everything by himself.' Just thinking about him makes me want to barf! After all, it's not so hard to ride a horse like that! I'd like to see how Mr. Lex handles the training of a young horse!"

Kevin had gotten himself all worked up, and Cathy really didn't want to talk about it anymore. But she was upset, too, and she only increased Kevin's anger when she said, without thinking, "I don't understand Ricki. After all, you two are going together. It's not right for her to flirt with other guys. If I had a boyfriend, I wouldn't even look at anybody else."

"Right," Kevin snarled. "And anyway, it's all Josh's fault! If he and Lillian –"

"You can't say that," Cathy cut him off. "It's not his fault if Ricki and Lex –" Cathy was trying to defend Lillian's boyfriend, but Kevin wouldn't let her finish.

"Oh, c'mon, stop it! I don't care about any of it anyway! In the future, Ricki can just stay away from me. She can do whatever she wants with this cowboy masquerade. See if I care! It is completely over between us! Finito!"

Cathy had never seen Kevin so angry. "Don't you want to

think about it some more?" she asked cautiously. "After all, nothing happened between the two of them, except that Ricki rode Charon and Lex rode Diablo."

"Ha!" exploded Kevin, his eyes flashing angrily. "You didn't see how she looked at him! I'm not an idiot!" Yet while he was saying these things, Kevin's thoughts were going in another direction.

Oh, please, I don't want to lose Ricki. I care for her so much ... It just can't be true, that she ... that she and that ... Lex. It makes me totally crazy just thinking that she might not want to be with me anymore.

"Kevin –"

"Cathy, just leave me alone!"

The boy shortened his hold on Sharazan's reins while pressing his heels into the horse's belly. The roan suddenly raced off at a fast trot.

Cathy was just able to keep Rashid from following his stall mate. Nevertheless, after Kevin had ridden quite a distance on Sharazan, she let the dun break into a gallop. While Rashid raced along, tears began to run down Cathy's cheeks.

The party could have been so much fun, she thought sadly. *Now it looks like our group's friendship is breaking completely apart. I always thought that love brought people together, not separated them. Apparently I was mistaken.*

*

When Ricki heard the old man scream, she turned as white as a sheet.

39

She spun around and stared at the house. At first she had thought it was empty, but now it seemed more like a haunted house out of a movie.

Diablo was scared, too, and Ricki could see the reins strain as he tried to free himself. She ran over to him as fast as she could, and managed to calm him down so that he stood still.

But the little pony wasn't frightened. She raised her muzzle toward the farmhouse and whinnied excitedly. Finally! Finally – after so long – she had heard her owner's voice again, but where was he? Why was he leaving her all alone, and why hadn't she been allowed to go into the stall for weeks now?

"Diablo, stay calm, boy. Nothing is going to happen to you! I promise. Hey, there really is someone in there!"

At that moment, the man's voice could be heard again, but this time it had a more whiny tone. Ricki had to listen closely to understand any of the words that were muted by the thick walls of the house.

"Salina, my little Salina, they can't take you away! Do you hear me? You have to stay here ... here."

Ricki had goose bumps all along her spine. Almost as though she was looking for protection, she moved closer to Diablo and pressed herself against his neck.

Who in the world was Salina? Where did someone want to take her? Was she a child or a –?

Ricki swallowed nervously. She continued to listen intently, but now there was nothing but silence.

Slowly, Ricki crawled over to a window to look inside. She was so tense that she almost screamed when there was a dull thud followed by someone whimpering.

What's happening in there? she wondered. She hurried from one window to the next, hoping to discover something.

Suddenly, she jerked back.

"Oh my gosh! Someone's lying on the floor in there," she whispered – pale as a ghost – as she discovered Hiram Parker. He had fallen while trying to get up from his bed. Now he lay on the wooden floor, unable to move at all.

Ricki took several deep breaths before she could make herself knock on the window, but the old man didn't seem to hear her.

"Hello! ... HELLO! Are you okay?" Ricki was knocking on the windowpane so hard that she was afraid it would break. She continued to call loudly, but the man didn't react to her words.

"I have to get in there," she mumbled to herself. "Somehow. If something has happened to this man, I can't just ride away and leave him here by himself. There has to be an open window somewhere."

Ricki took a few steps backward and looked along the side of the house. But she didn't see any way of getting inside. Quickly she ran around the house and tried to lift all of the windows. She even tried to open the front door, but everything was locked.

Resigned, she ran back to Diablo.

The fear that was spreading through her was making it difficult for her to breathe. Why did she have to be out riding alone today, of all days?

Meanwhile, Diablo kept kicking against the bottom of the two-piece stable door. All of a sudden, Ricki had an idea.

41

In many old farmhouses, there was often an entryway into the house from the barn, so maybe ... just maybe she would be lucky and there would be a door that was unlocked.

Ricki raced into the barn. "Be good, my boy," she pleaded with Diablo. "I'll be right back. Please, stand still."

After her eyes had become accustomed to the dark inside the barn, she quickly found the connecting door she'd been looking for. Her hands were trembling as she turned the knob. She closed her eyes in fear as the door opened, screeching, but with no problem.

Her knees shaking, the girl stepped inside the old man's house.

The air was stale. Ricki felt sick as she raced from one room to the next until – finally – she found Hiram Parker.

He lay motionless on the floor. Only his frightened eyes – which swung back and forth continuously – moved. When he saw Ricki, his face turned pale. Scared, he reached his hands out toward the girl in a defensive gesture.

"Don't shoot. Please don't shoot," he pleaded.

Oh no, he's completely insane, went through Ricki's head. Automatically, she stepped backward.

"Don't shoot!" the old man whimpered again. Suddenly Ricki realized what might be the cause of his fear.

Her outfit – the Stetson and the leather vest she was still wearing – may have reminded the old man of some old-time Western movie he'd seen. It was sending him into a panic.

Quickly, she took off the hat and flung the vest away.

"Don't be afraid. I just want to help you," she said softly.

"Horse thief! Salina is staying here! Go away!" screamed

42

the old man so loudly that Ricki's blood seemed to freeze in her veins. The man was so spooky, that although he didn't seem able to get up on his own, she was afraid to go near him.

She ran out of the room and supported herself against the wall in desperation. She closed her eyes for a few seconds and tried to collect her thoughts. It was clear that the man urgently needed help. However, since she didn't know her way around the area, it didn't make sense to just take off with Diablo to try to find a neighbor.

I wonder if there's a telephone here? Ricki thought. She forced herself to open her eyes.

"Stay calm," she said softly. She then began to search each room systematically for a telephone.

"I have more luck than brains." She breathed a sigh of relief when she finally found an ancient telephone in the kitchen among dozens of opened and unopened cans of mushrooms, among other pieces of trash.

With her hands shaking, she picked up the huge, heavy black receiver and dialed 911.

"Yeah, hello. This is Ricki Sulai. I'm here – uh-oh, I don't know where I am exactly – but there's an old man here lying on the floor and he can't get up. He seems to be confused. I ... What? No, I don't know the man. Wait, his name is ... just a minute ... okay, Hiram Parker. The address? No, I don't know, but there are some letters lying around. Maybe I'll find an address on one of them. Yeah, good, I'll hurry." Ricki threw down the receiver and raced through the barn and back outside, where she started going through the old man's mail with shaky hands.

She immediately found something and ran back inside.

"I have it!" she screamed into the telephone before giving the address. Right afterward, she set the receiver down weakly. The friendly woman on the line had promised that someone was coming immediately and told her to wait there.

Ricki forced herself to go back into the room where the old man was still lying on the cold wooden floor. He hadn't moved.

"Help is coming right away," Ricki whispered to him.

"Salina ... she belongs to me. Don't you dare touch my pony!" Parker's voice now sounded a lot weaker than when he had yelled at Ricki. The girl sensed that it might be better to get out of his sight so that he wouldn't get so upset.

Slowly, Ricki went back outside through the front door. She felt drained of energy as she walked back to the barn. It was like she had lead weights tied to her feet.

With her heart beating wildly, she leaned against Diablo and looked across at the pony mare.

"Her name is Salina," said Ricki softly. In her mind, she saw only the old man – lying on the floor – with his eyes wide open in fear.

*

Only a few minutes had gone by when Ricki noticed an ambulance approaching on the road. It was speeding toward the isolated farmhouse.

The girl breathed a sigh of relief. Excitedly, she began to wave both arms so that the driver wouldn't miss the farm's driveway.

A few minutes later, without saying much, the EMS driver had Ricki take him to the old man.

"The way he looks, he wouldn't have lasted much longer," said one of the paramedics when she saw the fragile old man.

Ricki turned aside, disgusted by what she had just heard. She couldn't understand how someone could talk like that in front of the old man. She watched with compassion as the EMS workers got him onto a stretcher and then into the ambulance. The doors were closed behind the EMS doctor.

"Please, give me your address," requested the driver. He held out a small tablet and a pen.

The girl wrote down her address, in a shaky hand, and then asked, "What's going to happen to him now?" .

"First, he'll be taken to a hospital, and then we'll see. I'm not authorized to tell you anymore than that." He put the writing pad and pen into his jacket pocket and then got into the vehicle.

"And what about Salina, the pony?" called Ricki.

"That's none of our business! We're not responsible for that!" was the immediate reply. Then the ambulance drove off and disappeared from view.

"That's the easy way out! The best thing is to not be responsible for anything!" Ricki stamped her foot, furious. She was completely unnerved and could hardly think straight.

She had hoped so much that the arrival of the ambulance would solve all of her problems. But now? Now she had another one by the name of Salina!

Ricki felt as though her legs couldn't carry her anymore, so she sat down for a few minutes. She peered over at the pony that stood all alone in the paddock.

"I can't just leave you here all by yourself," she said softly in Salina's direction. "But what will my parents say if I bring you home with me? I wish Kevin were here. He'd know what to do with you."

Ricki hesitated. Did she just say "Kevin"?

In the heat of the moment, she'd forgotten about Kevin's silly fit of jealousy, but now when she thought about Kevin, Lex automatically came to mind. It occurred to her to ride back to the clearing and ask the club members if they knew of anyone who had room for Salina.

But as she looked at the pony, which had come closer, she began to reconsider. And when the pony started to whinny softly and looked at her with huge dark eyes, that settled it. Ricki got up and walked over to the barn. "Diablo, we're taking the pony with us! I don't have any idea if we'll be able to keep her, but I'm not going to leave her here!"

Determined, she pushed past her horse and found an old calf rope to use as a lead. Now the only question was whether the pony would allow itself to be caught.

Then Ricki remembered Charon and Lex's demonstration of the "cutting" technique. That would really be practical right now. Charon could cut Salina off and – Ricki ran back to the paddock.

"Come here, little Salina," Ricki called softly as she walked slowly toward the pony. "You saw that your owner has been taken away, and it looks like you've been standing

46

out here for a long time. It's time to get you into a real stall. How would you like that, hmm?"

The pony perked up its ears attentively and overcame its initial fear. It kept watching Ricki's every move, and the girl was glad to see that Salina didn't look as though she were getting ready to run away.

"That's good, my little pony. Stand still. I only want to help you." Very slowly, Ricki moved forward a step at a time until she had gotten so close to the animal that all she had to do was stretch out her arm and grab the worn halter.

Just as Ricki started to make a grab for it, Diablo whinnied loudly. Salina turned back – frightened – and walked a few yards away. She stopped again.

"Great, Diablo! Thanks a lot. You couldn't have chosen a worse time to whinny! Darn it!" Ricki had turned around and given her horse a dirty look before beginning the same game of tag all over again. Altogether, it took Ricki five more attempts before she'd tied her rope to Salina's halter.

"I never would have thought it would be so difficult to catch a little pony," panted Ricki, out of breath. Lovingly, she stroked Salina's muzzle and then led her to the paddock gate, which seemed to be the only part of the fence still intact.

Ricki opened the gate and brought Salina over to Diablo, who looked at his owner with astonishment.

While holding onto Salina with one hand, Ricki used the other hand to screw the bit back in. She untied Diablo's reins before closing and locking the stall door.

"So," she said, looking at the animals with a smile. "Let's get going! I think it will be quite a while before we're back home." She took Diablo with her right hand and Salina with her left, and they all three started walking home.

Diablo had to walk really slowly, while Salina had to hurry in order for them to stay together.

Ricki was relieved to see that there didn't seem to be any injury to the pony's front leg. She walked down the trail toward the road and then turned right, the way the ambulance had gone. If that was the way to the hospital, then it was also the way back home.

Softly, Ricki began to whistle, "Home on the Range," while she listened to the rhythm of the hooves. It would take her more than an hour to get home on foot, she realized. *Walking for that length of time in riding boots will probably give me blisters all over my feet*, Ricki thought, groaning, but the main thing was that Salina was going to have a roof over her head.

I hope Mom doesn't make a big deal out of this, the girl thought, although right at that moment, even a fight with her mother didn't seem that important. Lovingly, Ricki stroked little Salina on the neck while the pony walked beside her obediently.

"Don't worry, Jake is there, too. He won't leave you standing outside in the rain," she said to Salina. With new resolve, she stopped talking and kept walking straight ahead.

*

Lillian had stayed at the party only an hour longer. During the barrel-racing contest, when they had to ride around three barrels as fast as possible along a designated track, she had watched nervously – standing first on one leg and then on the other with fingers crossed for good luck – as Josh, astride Cherish, competed with the others.

But Lex and Charon left them all in the dust.

Lex directed his horse through the square testing area without reining him in. Here were some equestrian acrobatics, and there was a change in direction – all done without the reins. Lex was able to guide his horse just by the pressure of his thighs or by changing his weight. Every once in a while, he used his voice as well. The highlight of his performance was when he stopped Charon short during a full gallop! Lex held his arms crossed in front of his chest. He had proven how unnecessary it was to give signals with the reins. His performance was greeted with thunderous applause.

As interesting as it was, Lillian had known no peace of mind ever since her friends had left the party without saying anything.

"Please don't be mad at me if I go home now, too," she said to Josh. "I've got a bad feeling. I think something may be wrong at home."

"Oh, come on. If your friends behave like kindergarteners, that's not your problem. Is it?" Josh couldn't hide his disappointment at Lillian's plan to leave early. "I was really looking forward to spending the whole day with you."

Lillian kissed him on the cheek and smiled lovingly at him. "I sincerely hope that there will be other days when we'll be together, don't you?"

"Hmm," murmured Josh with some resignation, while he accompanied his girlfriend to her Doc Holliday. "Well, then, take care and see that you get everything straightened out with those jealous adolescents!"

Lillian nodded and mounted. "See you," she said. "You have really nice friends. And the party was great!"

"The best is yet to come. Afterward, we're going to –"

"Josh!" Lillian looked at him pleadingly.

"All right, all right, I get it. I know you won't change your mind."

"Okay, see you tomorrow. Or can you come by the stables later?"

"Maybe," said Josh. "It depends on how long we stay here."

Lillian nodded. She blew her boyfriend a kiss, and called goodbye to Lex and Gringo before she rode off on Holli.

*

Cathy and Kevin were still in the stable when Lillian arrived with Doc Holliday. While she was leading her horse to his stall, the fifteen-year-old could sense the sizzling tension that was coming from her two friends.

"I didn't feel like staying after you guys all took off," Lillian explained. "You could have at least said something! Josh was looking for you –"

"Then you left Ricki alone at the party. Well, she'll have a free hand with her Lex, anyway," announced Kevin, grinding his teeth.

Lillian rolled her eyes. "I said that I wasn't in the mood to stay because *all* of you had left! Maybe you need to listen more closely when someone says something."

"Don't you get on my case, too," replied Kevin angrily. His brain was working overtime. Ricki had ridden off too? But then, she should have been back ages ago, unless ... unless she was riding with Lex somewhere.

Lillian seemed able to read his thoughts. "No! She is *not* with Lex. He's probably still riding around the training area on Charon!" she said. She unsaddled Holli and started brushing him.

"Where is she then?"

"How should I know?" asked Lillian. "I thought that I'd find all three of you here. At the very worst, I could have played referee if you'd gotten into a fight!"

"Hey, what's that supposed to mean!" Now Cathy was upset, too. She gave Lillian a dirty look.

"You know what? Josh was right! You're both acting like little kids after someone has taken away their ball! Don't you realize how ridiculous you're acting?"

Cathy and Kevin didn't say anything.

"You two are jealous for absolutely no reason," said Lillian seriously. "All Ricki and Lex did was exchange rides on each other's horses and talk. Is that a crime, or what?"

"Didn't you see how they were looking at each other? That said it all." Kevin could not be comforted.

"Are they supposed to keep their eyes closed while they're talking? How can you be so jealous? If Josh acted the way you're acting whenever I talked to other guys, it would be all over between us! Our relationship would be ruined."

"Yeah, thought so!" Kevin thought he saw his suspicions confirmed by Lillian's words.

"Kevin, you are an idiot. You haven't understood anything I've tried to tell you," Lillian said, shaking her head. "It's no use talking to you."

"But he's right," piped up Cathy. Lillian cut her off immediately.

"How can you judge that? Just because you have a crush on Lex – which he apparently doesn't share – now you're mad at Ricki. And you haven't even given her a chance to say anything about this! You two are so childish it's unbelievable!" Lillian left Holli's stall and threw the brush angrily into her grooming basket.

"Since you're so grown up –" Cathy started to say.

"Oh, shut up, both of you! I'd have been better off staying at the party!"

"No one asked you to chase after us," said Kevin, He leaned against the stall wall, his arms crossed on his chest stubbornly.

Lillian brought her basket into the tack room before leaving the stable. She looked all around, trying to catch a glimpse of Ricki or Diablo, but there was no sign of them anywhere.

I just hope nothing has happened, she thought as she kept glancing at her watch. *Maybe Kevin is right. Maybe Ricki met Lex somewhere.*

"If she did, then there's going to be a real fight between the two of them when she gets back," Lillian murmured to herself, as she sat down on the sun-warmed gravel. She'd planned to go home and get into a warm bath, but instead she decided to wait there until Ricki returned.

Chapter 4

Ricki's feet were beginning to blister and her arm was becoming stiff from leading Salina. The weak pony walked in an irregular manner. Sometimes Ricki had to use force to pull her forward, but when a car approached, she'd start galloping away in fright.

At last! Ricki – completely exhausted – heaved a huge sigh of relief when she caught sight of the roof of her house in the distance.

"I'll be so happy to get home," she said to the two horses just as a truck approached them from behind.

"Not again," she groaned. "I'm getting it from all sides today!"

As quickly as she could, she pulled the horses into the meadow and held them still, with their heads facing the road.

"Don't do anything stupid," she warned Salina, as she shortened the rope while holding on to the halter. Ricki wasn't worried about Diablo. He was used to all kinds of vehicles and could be depended on not to spook in traffic.

"Stand still," Ricki pleaded with the pony as the truck came closer.

About ten yards before the driver caught up to the horses, he honked his horn and grinned broadly, then thundered right by the animals.

That was too much even for Diablo. Frightened, he reared up on his hind legs. Ricki had to let go of the pony in order to calm him.

"Diablo, stop ... calm down. Whoa, Diablo, stand still. Oh no! Salina, come back ... Saliiiinaaaa ... " Ricki could have wept. She was angry and frustrated, but worse, she was worried about the safety of the frightened pony. She leapt into the saddle, and she and Diablo, happy to stretch his muscles, raced after the pony.

They caught up with Salina quickly, but Ricki had a hard time getting Diablo to stop. The black horse wanted to gallop around the meadow a little longer.

Salina ran across the meadow in zigzag patterns, like a scared rabbit. Ricki was worried that she might get her hooves caught in the rope, which was hanging down dangerously near her legs.

Suddenly the girl remembered Lex and Charon. They would have known how to catch the pony!

Maybe I should ride around in an arc and then come straight toward her, thought Ricki, while Diablo raced directly behind Salina.

The little mare became panic-stricken at being chased, and once again, made an abrupt change in the direction in which she was going.

Ricki was frightened and tried to stop Diablo, but at the

last moment Salina ran right into his legs. The horse stumbled and fell, his rider still in the saddle.

Ricki screamed and landed on the ground, having flown over Diablo's neck. She remained lying there for a few horrible minutes; her wrist began to throb with pain.

*

Lex left the party shortly after Lillian's departure.

"Do you have any plans for tonight?" asked Josh. Like Lex, he was usually one of the last to leave the club gatherings.

"Who knows?" his friend answered with a twinkle in his eyes as he swung himself onto Charon. "See you later," he called to him, and then he waved goodbye with his Stetson before he and Charon galloped out of sight.

"O-ooo," said Josh, as he watched Lex ride away. "Don't do anything stupid, old buddy. Ricki is really much too young for you."

*

Lex wanted to enjoy a little peace and quiet before riding home to study for an exam scheduled for the next day. It was important to him to get his career off to a good start, and he had planned to put in some serious study time that evening.

He gave Charon a loose rein and let him gallop freely; Lex loved the feel of the warm wind on his face. He had turned onto an unfamiliar trail, but when he realized it, he just shrugged his shoulders and rode on. This trail would take him home, too.

He reveled in these moments of complete freedom. Maybe someday he would ride through an endless prairie landscape, or through a canyon, or …

What's going on over there? Lex was abruptly torn from his daydream. He reined in Charon to a halt and squinted in order to see what was happening in the distance in front of him.

He saw a truck. He could even hear its horn beeping, and then he thought he saw a horse bolt away, but he wasn't completely sure.

"C'mon, Charon, let's have a closer look." He said softly and urged the horse into a gallop.

*

"Are you waiting for Josh?" Jake, who was just walking by the stalls, asked Lillian.

"Why do you ask?" the fifteen-year-old looked up at the stable hand and wondered.

"Well, because you're so jumpy. You're only like that when you're waiting for your boyfriend!"

Lillian rolled her eyes. At the moment, she wasn't in the mood for jokes.

"Where's Diablo?" called Jake, as he realized that the stall of his beloved horse was empty.

"That's why I'm so upset. Ricki should have been home long ago," admitted Lillian cautiously, because she knew that Jake would be worried sick when he found out.

"That's what I thought. How come you didn't ride back together? Did you guys get into a fight again?"

56

"What do you mean, 'again'? We don't fight that often," Lillian corrected him, but Jake just shook his head.

They'll make up again, he thought to himself, *they always do*. It was more important to him that Diablo and Ricki get home safe and sound.

"They'll probably be here soon," Lillian was trying to comfort herself as well as the stable hand. Meanwhile, Cathy and Kevin sat in a corner of the tack room and talked about the topic that was still bothering them: Lex and Ricki.

*

Lex and Charon approached the spot where the truck had frightened Ricki's horses. Up ahead he could see Diablo and an unfamiliar pony, but where was Ricki?

"Uh-oh, this doesn't look good at all! Let's go, Charon, show me your stuff!" Lex pressed his heels lightly into Charon's belly. The animal reacted immediately to the signal and raced over the meadow toward the place where Ricki lay on the ground.

"Whoa, Charon!" yelled Lex. Even before his horse had come to a complete stop, Lex had jumped down from the saddle and was kneeling beside Ricki in an instant.

"Hey, how are you doing? Are you okay?" he asked.
Ricki nodded. "For the most part, yes, I think so. Could you please take care of Diablo and the pony?"

Lex nodded, although at the moment he was much more concerned about Ricki.

With a glance at Ricki, he got up slowly and turned toward

the animals. Diablo was standing near Ricki, his muzzle lowered into the wonderfully fragrant grass, but Salina kept her gaze on Lex. He spoke softly to her, but when he tried to get closer, she kept moving to the side, out of his reach. It seemed impossible to get to her.

So Lex focused on catching Diablo's reins and leading him over to Ricki.

"The fall doesn't seem to have injured those two. Can you hold Diablo?" he asked with a glance at her swollen wrist.

Seeing his concern, Ricki said, "It's okay," but she was still a little shaky.

She held Diablo's reins in her uninjured hand. "Her name is Salina," Ricki called after him.

"Come here, little Salina," Lex coaxed the pony mare. "What's wrong? Are you afraid of people? You're so cute. You could be a little fatter, maybe, and you could stand to be brushed, but otherwise I think you're terrific!"

Salina seemed comforted by Lex's calming voice, but when he came closer, she ran away again.

"Charon!" Lex commanded his horse to come to him and the horse obeyed instantly. Lex knotted the open reins together over the horse's neck, to prevent them from falling, stroked him a bit, and then he said, "Go, Charon, bring her to me!"

He pointed to Salina with his outstretched arms and then gave his horse a light slap.

Charon understood. He immediately started moving in a large circle around the little mare until he stopped way behind her.

"That's good, Charon. Now, bring her here, okay?" Lex

nodded encouragingly to his horse and Charon began to move toward the pony.

Salina's head swung around. She kept looking, back and forth at Charon and Lex, as though trying to figure out which one of them would be easier to escape from.

Lex stood a few yards in front of her and held out his arms, blocking her route straight ahead. Charon came at her from behind, and he didn't look as though he was going to let her get past him.

Salina didn't hesitate for a minute. She bolted to the right to run away, but she hadn't counted on Charon's quick response time.

Charon had had sufficient training in the cutting technique to know how to act. With one jump on his hind legs, he turned in the direction of Salina's escape path and cut her off. With his two front legs wide apart, and his head somewhat low, he stood in front of the little mare and stared at her.

Salina shook her shaggy mane angrily and tried again, but no matter which direction she turned, Charon was always a little bit faster than she was and wouldn't allow her to get by him.

Slowly, Charon approached the little mare and guided her backward toward Lex, who had only to wait for the right moment to grab her halter.

Ricki watched, her eyes bright with fascination. Charon's performance had so distracted her that she even forgot about her pain. He really was a magnificent horse. And she was pleased when she realized that her plan for catching the pony had been exactly right.

Diablo poked her gently, but Ricki was so taken by Charon's skillful maneuvers that she paid him little attention.

"Have you ever seen anything like that before?" she asked him, shaking her head in amazement.

"Success!" called Lex after a few minutes. He raised his hand triumphantly, holding Salina's rope. "Good boy," he praised Charon, patting his neck proudly. "You did a great job! You're my best horse!" Then he brought Salina to Ricki.

"So, we have the little lady again. Is she yours?"

Ricki shook her head no. "It's a long story," she sighed.

"Tell me what happened," Lex asked, but before Ricki could begin, he held up his hand. "Wait, where were you headed? Do you live around here?"

The girl pointed to the roof in the distance. "It isn't very far, but on foot, it seems much farther." She smiled awkwardly.

"Why on foot?" Lex looked at her, astonished. "Why don't you ride Charon? He's used to one-handed neck reining, and I'll come beside you with these two heroes. Okay?" He didn't even wait for Ricki's answer. He just helped her into the saddle.

"So! Everything okay? Oh, wait a minute. I have to untie the reins," laughed Lex. Ricki realized that she liked his laughter more and more.

"So, good, then let's go. Does that hurt a lot?"

"It's okay," lied Ricki.

"I read you loud and clear! It really hurts!" guessed Lex.

"Do you want to hear Salina's story or not?" asked Ricki, changing the subject.

Lex smiled up at her. "You're tough, aren't you? Fine, go ahead and tell me the story. I can't wait to hear how you found this skinny little shaggy creature," he said, but he looked at Salina with so much tenderness that Ricki's heart skipped a beat.

He's going to be a good and compassionate vet, she thought to herself. Then she began the story of how she met Hiram Parker.

*

"Well, good for you, Ricki. Mr. Parker probably owes you his life!" exclaimed Lex after hearing Ricki's story. "That would be a good human-interest article for our boring local newspaper. Now, what's going to happen to this here little pony?"

Ricki shrugged her shoulders. "No idea. Like I said, no one's taking any responsibility! At first I thought I'd take her home with me. She might be a good companion for Lillian's little donkey, Chico. That would be perfect. The two of them could share a stall. It's big enough, and Chico wouldn't be so lonely when we go out riding on the horses."

"What do you think your parents will say to all this?" Lex wanted to know, but Ricki wouldn't answer that.

"I think – before I start imagining anything – I'll just let them surprise me. There are only two possibilities."

"Well, maybe your parents will be okay with this. You only need to find temporary housing for the pony."

"What do you mean 'temporary housing'?" asked Ricki, confused.

"Well, at some point, Mr. Parker will get out of the hospital. Then he'll want his pony back, right?"

Ricki looked at Salina for a long time. "I guess so. I didn't think that far ahead! But I agree with you. I think she's really cute. I think I could get used to her."

"Of course you could! So, is that your farm over there?" Lex looked ahead with interest.

"Yes!" Ricki was surprised at how quickly the time had passed and how easily they had managed the distance.

"It's nice here," he said, surveying the area. "And your friends are here, too."

"Where?" Ricki raised her head, but Kevin and Cathy had already disappeared into the stables. Only Lillian stared at them, her mouth wide open.

"Oh, no!" groaned Lillian. "She's coming with Lex, and sitting in Charon's saddle no less. Argh! If only I had decided on the bath instead." Then she noticed the little pony that Lex was leading into the yard along with Diablo.

"Hey, Lily," Ricki greeted her, a little embarrassed.

"I've asked you not to call me that," her girlfriend answered. "What are you doing here and where did you get the pony?" she wanted to know from Lex. He answered by handing her both Diablo's reins and Salina's rope.

"Here, can you hold these for a minute?" he asked. Then he ran over to Charon to help Ricki down from the saddle.

After sitting motionless in the saddle for so long, every bone in Ricki's body ached.

"You should put your arm in a sling right away, or even better, get a doctor to look at it," said Lex sympathetically, and only then did Lillian realize that there was something wrong with Ricki.

"Did something happen?"

"Nothing serious." Ricki tried to play it down. She asked Lillian to take Diablo and the pony into the stable.

In the meantime, Lex had swung up into Charon's saddle.

"I'm going to head home, then," he said with an encouraging smile at Ricki. "I've got an exam to study for."

"Thanks for everything, Lex. Maybe sometime I can return the favor," she said quietly. She was really sorry that the young man had to leave so soon.

"I'll come visit you," Lex promised with a tip of his finger against the brim of his Stetson. He turned his beautiful horse elegantly on a back leg and rode off toward home.

Ricki is a really nice girl, he thought, and looked back one more time. *Kevin should be glad to have her as a girlfriend.* Then he urged Charon into a gallop and disappeared quickly from view.

*

"What's that?" asked Cathy, puzzled, as Lillian brought little Salina into the stable beside Diablo.

"Maybe a pony?" replied Ricki, who had also come into the stall. *What a stupid question*, she thought to herself.

"Yeah, it's obviously a pony, but where'd it come from? And what are you going to do with it?" Cathy's voice sounded a little hurt, but before Ricki could answer, Kevin came walking over to them.

Disappointed, he looked at her as he spoke: "I was right, after all, wasn't I? That guy is your type! Do you think it's all right just to dump me like this? You even let him bring you home! Well, at least you got rid of that ridiculous outfit."

"Oh, yeah, the hat and the vest. Darn, I forgot all about them. Pepe will be furious with me!" groaned Ricki and smacked her forehead with her healthy hand.

"Is that all you have to say?" Kevin's eyes narrowed to slits. "Did that wannabe vet dazzle you so much you can't even ride your own horse anymore? You know what I think about someone who steals someone else's girlfriend?"

"That's enough, Kevin!" Ricki looked at him angrily. "You're way out of line! Diablo and I fell just as Lex was riding by. He and Charon helped me catch the pony. He could see that I was in pain from the fall so he let me ride Charon while he led Salina and Diablo home." As proof, she tried to raise her swollen arm, but it hurt so much that she got tears in her eyes.

"You have no idea what happened because you rode home in a jealous fit with Cathy!" sobbed Ricki. She pushed Kevin away.

"Lillian, do you think we could put Salina in Chico's stall?" she asked her girlfriend, wiping away her tears.

"We can try," responded Lillian, putting Diablo's reins into Cathy's hand. Then she led Salina over to Chico.

Curious, the little donkey stuck his nose over the sides of the stall and wiggled his long ears back and forth.

Salina looked at the gray donkey somewhat skeptically at first, but then she decided she liked him. She snorted softly at him, and when Ricki opened the gate a little, she pushed right past her and went inside.

"Slowly, slowly," Lillian cautioned. "I have to see if you two can get along." But Chico and the pony seemed to have already made some kind of secret pact with each other.

Willingly, the donkey stepped aside and welcomed the little mare.

Ricki and Lillian observed the two for a few minutes, just to be sure, but the two of them – so different from each other – seemed to get along perfectly.

"Could you please put an armful of hay into the hayrack?" Ricki begged her girlfriend. "The little pony hasn't had anything decent to eat for a long time."

"Of course!" Lillian opened a bale of hay and carried an armful over to Chico and Salina, who began to eat ravenously. The pony, her hunger satisfied, kept looking gratefully at Lillian.

"I think we can just leave them alone," she said, locking the stall gate securely.

Ricki had gone over to Diablo as Cathy was unsaddling him.

"Thanks for your help," said Ricki softly, but Cathy just pressed her lips together and disappeared into the tack room without saying anything.

"Where did you get the pony?" Lillian wanted to know. She looked at Ricki anxiously.

"That would interest me as well."

"Me, too!"

Unnoticed by the others, Jake and Brigitte Sulai, Ricki's mother, had entered the stable. The elderly stable hand shook his head and looked back and forth between the girl and the pony.

"Uh-oh." Ricki tried to hide her swollen arm from her mother and put it behind her back, but it hurt too much. She groaned out loud.

"Good heavens, what happened to your arm? Don't tell me you fell off your horse!" Brigitte's eyes widened in horror. Once again, her suspicion that riding was a dangerous sport had been confirmed.

"You have to go to the doctor right away!" she ordered. Brigitte tried to pull Ricki along with her, but the girl resisted with all her strength.

"Please, you all wanted to know where the pony came from, so let me tell you. It was like this –"

"I don't care where it came from. It's not going to stay here!" Ricki's mother decided angrily. "I am not going to put up with any more of these dangerous animals!"

"But Salina isn't dangerous. She's sweet and she no longer has a home," Ricki tried to interrupt her mother, but Brigitte wasn't listening.

"Come on, let's go! I hope we can reach a doctor this late!"

"I don't want to go to a doctor!" yelled Ricki so loudly that the horses jerked in fright. "I want to tell you what happened! Do you think I just showed up with this completely strange pony for fun? I'm not that stupid! I knew there would be a scene! However, I can't take the pony back! Its owner is –" And once again, everything that had happened poured out of Ricki. Again she saw the old man on the floor in front of her, and she could still hear the voice of the emergency guy, "… not responsible …"

"I couldn't just leave Salina there alone, could I? Who would have looked after her? She would have starved to

66

death. Look at her! She's been terribly neglected! And she's so sweet. Mom, please understand this –" Ricki was completely exhausted, physically and emotionally. She leaned against Diablo's neck and sobbed into his coat.

I wish Lex were here, she thought, hardly noticing that Brigitte had put a hand onto her shoulder.

"Calm down, Ricki," she tried to comfort the girl. "Let's talk about this tomorrow, or at least later on, okay? That was a terrible thing you experienced today, but we still have to get Doctor Clemens to exam your arm – now! Okay?" Brigitte forced herself to be patient and guided Ricki gently but firmly toward the stable door.

Suddenly, Kevin stood in front of them and, chagrined, gazed at Ricki.

"Ricki, I ... I'm so sorry about ... well, you know what I mean," he stammered, but his girlfriend just shook her head sadly.

"Just leave me alone, okay?!" Ricki exploded. She walked past him quickly. It was all Brigitte could do to keep up with her daughter as she strode angrily out of the stable.

Chapter 5

Dr. Clemens – who was familiar with Ricki's penchant for getting scrapes and bruises – examined her arm carefully. He determined it to be just sprained, not broken; painful, but not serious.

"In a few days, I'll be good as new," Ricki beamed at her mother as she came out of the doctor's office. She had to admit she was glad her mother had insisted on taking her to the doctor. Her arm still hurt, but it was a great relief to know that it would get better soon.

Brigitte got up from her chair and embraced her daughter. "That's great news. I feel so much better now that we've gotten Doctor Clemens' diagnosis. Now, let's go home."

In the car, on the drive back to the farm, Ricki decided to risk bringing up the subject of the pony again. "Mom," she began timidly, "can Salina stay with us?"

Brigitte didn't answer, but the expression on her face said, "No." She was afraid of horses, and she was always terribly nervous when Ricki went riding.

It was a different story with Marcus, Ricki's father. Before Jake had given Diablo into Ricki's care and keeping, Marcus had been unable to understand the intense interest that Ricki and her friends had in horses. Now that Diablo was a regular member of the household, he understood and shared Ricki's love of the large, gentle animals. He wasn't quite as crazy about them as his daughter was, but every time he went to the stable or walked past the paddock, he always had a little something in his pocket for the horses. He loved to spoil them, and he always stroked them and talked kindly to them.

"Mom, please!" Ricki pleaded again.

"Ricki, you know I'm uneasy around horses. I'm going to need some time to think it over," her mother replied in an even tone.

I have to talk with Dad about this, the girl thought, staring straight ahead at the street. *Salina just has to stay home with us! I won't let her be taken to an animal shelter!*

Brigitte drove her daughter home without further conversation. When she turned into the driveway, she saw Carlotta Mancini's car parked outside. Carlotta, Rashid's owner, a retired circus performer, came by at least once a day to check on the animals.

Ricki sighed with relief. Carlotta was absolutely crazy about horses, and was sure to put in a good word for Salina with Ricki's parents.

The girl got out of the car quickly and ran to the stalls, where – just as she had suspected – Carlotta was standing in front of Chico's stall on the crutches she had needed ever since a terrible circus performing accident years before.

With her were Ricki's friends and Jake. They were talking about Salina.

Lillian had told Carlotta all about Ricki's encounter with Hiram Parker and why she had tried to rescue the pony. The older woman had understood completely.

"She did the right thing!" Carlotta was saying. "This poor animal really needs some care and attention. Don't you think so, Jake? It wouldn't take long to put some meat on those bones!"

"Well, Chico has thrived under my care," bragged the stable hand, before he reminded them how thin the little donkey had been when it had arrived at the stable some months ago.

"Hello, Carlotta," called Ricki, glad to see Rashid's owner. "Isn't Salina sweet? Mom is having her usual fit and doesn't want to let her stay here. Could you talk to her? I –"

"Hi, Ricki. How are you? Lillian tells me you and Diablo took a nasty fall. How's your arm?" Full of sympathy, Carlotta turned to the girl.

Ricki just waved it off. "Everything's fine. Doctor Clemens says it's just a sprain! Carlotta, what do you think? Can you help me work things out so that Salina can stay here?"

Carlotta – who early on had recognized Ricki's great love of horses – knew exactly what was going through the young girl's head.

"Well, we'll see what we can do!" Carlotta smiled encouragingly. Suddenly Ricki was sure that she didn't need to worry about where Salina was going to stay. Carlotta was really good at convincing people, and she had often succeeded in changing Brigitte's mind.

"You're the greatest!" yelled Ricki, relieved. She gave Carlotta a big hug.

*

Cathy and Kevin had stepped to the side in embarrassment when Ricki entered the stable. Now they were standing with their horses, uncertain about how to act around her. Of course, Carlotta noticed immediately that something was wrong between them. She gave them a quizzical look.

"Do I sense tension here?" she asked after observing them for a while. No one answered. "Could it be that you kids are creating problems where there aren't any? That's not good! No matter what happens, kids, you can always talk it over! So, now I'm going to go find Brigitte. See you all later."

Jake was still standing in front of the stall, unable to take his eyes off Salina. He scratched his chin thoughtfully.

"I don't know. I just don't know. Something's wrong here. Thin on the top, but with such a huge belly. I think Doctor Hofer should have a look at her."

Ricki came closer, shocked.

"Do you think she's sick?" she asked Jake, who understood more about horses than most riders.

"Hmm," said Jake. "It's a possibility."

"Do you think I should have the vet come today?" asked Ricki anxiously.

"I'd wait one more day. Give the mare a chance to get used to her surroundings before she has to go through an examination."

71

"Then you don't think it's too serious!"

Jake became exasperated at Ricki's questions. "Girl, I don't know. I'm not a vet, but I can tell you one thing. She has a bad case of worms!"

"Darn! Does that mean Chico will get worms, too, if they stay together in the same stall?" Lillian had just joined them.

"I think, if Doctor Hofer comes tomorrow, that he should bring a worm cure for all of the horses and for Chico as well. Better safe than sorry!" Jake turned around to look at the big clock on the wall. "I still have time for a little nap before I have to get to work," he said before shuffling out of the stable. "Come on, Lupo, let's rest for a few minutes!" With some effort, Jake bent down and picked up the old tomcat that followed him around like a dog. The animal began to purr right away, as Jake carried him to his cottage on the Sulais' property.

Now that they were alone, the friends just stood there in awkward silence.

Ricki thought about what Carlotta had said: *You can talk anything over.* If only it were that easy. Desperately, she searched for a way to begin that wouldn't upset Kevin all over again.

"Ricki, I want to –"

"RICKI ... telephone." Brigitte Sulai interrupted Kevin by calling to her daughter from the kitchen window, "Somebody named Alex wants to speak to you! Are you coming?"

"Coming," Ricki called back. She ran past Kevin, who clenched his fists furiously.

"So that's that! It's clear now who's more important! I've had enough. I'm leaving! You can tell your girlfriend that we're through! That's final!" Kevin gave Lillian an angry look and stomped out without even saying goodbye to Sharazan.

Cathy swallowed hard. She glanced at the stable door through which the youth had just disappeared and said suddenly, "I think that's really mean, the way Ricki is acting! She can't do that to Kevin! I thought she cared for him."

Lillian rolled her eyes. "Are you out of your mind again? What did Ricki do that was so bad? She went to the telephone because she had gotten a call. Is that so terrible? Lex brought her here after all, and he probably just wants to know how she and Salina are doing! Kevin's the one who's acting weird! Cathy, wait a minute." Lillian ran after her friend, who had run out of the stable without letting her finish.

Outside, she watched as Cathy and Kevin got on their bikes and got ready to ride off. "What's going on? I thought we four were friends?" she called after them.

"That's what I thought, too, until a little while ago," Kevin replied nastily before pedaling away.

Cathy had trouble keeping up with him, but she wanted to stay with him. It wasn't so long ago that she'd had a crush on Kevin herself, but Ricki had the advantage every time.

Let her go to that Lex. Kevin is much nicer anyway, thought Cathy. She decided to do her best to win him for herself.

*

73

Lillian stayed behind, shaking her head. She wished Josh were here so that she could discuss the situation with him. *If I'd known the mess that party was going to stir up, I never would have taken the others to it*, she thought sadly. She walked slowly back to the stalls, her head hanging. Maybe Doc Holliday could comfort her.

*

Lex had only wanted to ask Ricki how she was feeling, and the telephone call was quickly over. However, Ricki – happy to hear his voice – had persuaded herself that she detected a special affectionate undertone in his words. When he said that he would come by soon and start training Diablo, her heart began beating wildly in anticipation of his promised visit.

Ricki walked out of the front door in a great mood but then stopped short, shocked to see a policeman getting out of his patrol car.

"Hello," the officer greeted her warmly. "I'm looking for a Ricki Sulai. Am I in the right place?"

Ricki nodded and suddenly she felt her knees grow weak for no particular reason.

"Yes, that's me. Hi!"

"Hello! My name is Officer Paul Stevenson. Can I talk to you for a minute? It's about the gentleman you found in his house today."

Ricki nodded again and asked the policeman to come inside.

"Police? Well, has something happened?" Carlotta asked as she and Brigitte were leaving the kitchen.

"Good afternoon, ladies. No, nothing has happened. I just have a few questions for Ricki. It's about Mr. Parker."

"Of course, come on in, please! Ricki's mother led Officer Stevenson into the living room and asked him to take a seat.

While Ricki told her story once again, Brigitte brought the officer a cup of coffee, which he accepted gladly.

"We got your address from the EMS driver. As always, if someone is found in mysterious circumstances, and without any relatives present, we have to investigate. It's always possible that his injuries were caused by someone else, or that someone had broken in and stolen something, or –"

Ricki had gone pale. "You don't think that I threw the old man out of bed and then stole something before I called 911, do you?" she asked heatedly.

The officer laughed. "To be honest, I don't think you could do something like that. But there is one thing that is really strange. The driver said that there had been a horse on the paddock, but when I drove by just now, I didn't see one. Do you know anything about that?"

Ricki's face changed colors, from white to red. "Yes. Salina is in our stable. I took her with me because nobody wanted to take responsibility for her. I couldn't just leave her there. I didn't steal her, though! I just wanted her to get fed. When Mr. Parker returns home, of course I'll bring her back. Honest! I just didn't want Salina being put away in some animal shelter! I –"

"Slowly, slowly, young lady! Can I see the animal?"

Ricki nodded and got up shakily. It made her uncomfortable to think that someone might have the idea that she'd stolen something, even if it had been for a good reason.

With the officer following behind her, Ricki walked slowly to the stables, where Lillian was still waiting for her.

"Ricki, Kevin and Cathy have – Oh, hello –" Lillian stopped herself in mid-sentence when she saw that her friend wasn't alone.

"Hello! So, where's the body?" the police officer asked, grinning and looking around. "These are really beautiful horses," he exclaimed admiringly. Ricki pointed wordlessly to the last stall, where Chico was peering over the top of the sides.

"That's not a pony, is it?"

"Oh no, that's Chico, my little donkey," replied Lillian before she realized that the officer had been trying to make a joke.

"Salina is in the stall with him," explained Ricki. She opened the sliding gate.

The visitor hesitated for a moment as he looked the animal over.

"I didn't steal Salina, but she was so starved for food –" began Ricki again, but the officer just waved his arm and closed the gate.

"I've seen enough," he said, nodding amicably at the girl. "I'm sure that the little horse is being well cared for here and that this stall is much better than an animal shelter. You know that yourself. Fine." He turned to Brigitte, who was standing in the doorway with Carlotta.

"It is really kind of you to take care of this animal until the real owner gets out of the hospital. However, it must be returned at that time. I'm sure the old gentleman will take good care of the pony when he is able to do so."

Brigitte's mouth opened and closed. Ricki knew what her mother actually wanted to say, but Mrs. Sulai remained silent.

Wordlessly, Ricki reached out her hand to say goodbye to the officer. "Ricki, I just want to tell you that there aren't very many young people your age who would have handled the situation as well as you did. That was really excellent! Take care. We'll be in touch again once Mr. Parker is discharged from the hospital." With those words, the police officer went back to his car and drove off.

"I guess it was meant to be," mumbled Brigitte, resigned. She smiled as Ricki gave her a spontaneous thank-you kiss on the cheek.

Carlotta winked at Ricki, her fellow conspirator.

"Where are Cathy and Kevin?" Ricki asked Lillian after the two women had retreated back into the house.

"Well – hmmm – how can I tell you this?" her friend stammered.

"What?"

"Well, Kevin asked me to tell you that he's breaking up with you, and Cathy was on his side. Lex's phone call –"

"Say that again. No, stop! Don't say anything! Kevin broke up with me? Because of Lex? But I – And Cathy agrees with him? ... That's unbelievable!" Ricki shook her head. Dejected, she slid down the wall on her back until she collapsed on the ground.

Without really seeing him, she focused on Diablo, who

was watching her attentively. He seemed to sense that something was wrong with his best friend.

"And ... and Cathy doesn't want anything to do with me either?" she asked softly and felt tears coming.

Lillian shrugged her shoulders. Without saying anything, she slid down beside Ricki. She put her arm around her friend and without a word, just held her tightly, as Ricki cried her heart out.

At this point, Ricki wasn't thinking about Lex at all. She was only thinking about Kevin, and how he would never be her friend again, and how much that hurt.

*

Ricki had a very bad night. She tossed and turned, while her thoughts went on a roller-coaster ride. When she finally fell asleep she had the most chaotic dreams, and woke up from them drenched with sweat, her heart beating wildly.

Exhausted, but glad that the night was over, Ricki forced herself out of bed early. She was in the stable before Jake.

"Good morning, my sweetheart," she greeted Diablo sadly, holding out a carrot for him. "Did you at least sleep well?" Of course, she didn't get an answer. Then she ran past all of the stalls to get a look at Salina, who was lying close to Chico on the ground. The pony looked up at her sleepily.

"Are you okay, little one?" asked Ricki quietly. "Stay where you are a little longer. It's still very early."

She began to fork hay into the animals' hayracks, which wasn't that easy, because her wrist was still hurting.

What a shame, thought Ricki. *I won't be able to do the*

mucking out for Jake this morning, and I really wanted to do something to take my mind off everything.

Driven by inner turmoil, she paced back and forth in the stable corridor. She kept looking outside every few minutes. She hoped that somehow Kevin would appear, put his arms around her, and tell her that yesterday had been a bad dream.

Downcast, Ricki crept back into the house and tiptoed upstairs to her room, where she threw herself across the bed. She missed Kevin terribly.

*

In the afternoon, Dr. Hofer, the vet, stood in the corridor in front of Salina's stall. He had just finished a complete examination of the little pony.

"Well, first of all, I'd say that this pony hasn't been sufficiently fed. Secondly, I suspect there's something wrong with her digestive tract. Look," he explained to Ricki, who was listening closely to everything he said, "the belly is swollen, and when you put your hands on it, you can actually feel the movement in the intestines. You can even hear a grumbling, which indicates poor fermentation in the digestive tract."

"And where can that have come from?" the girl wanted to know.

"Well, that can have several different causes. Rotten or impure hay that hasn't been stored long enough can cause poor fermentation, but so can warm or wet grass that has been lying in a pile for a certain length of time. Eating too much or too fast can also cause this or even colic."

79

"Well, since too much feed is definitely out of the question in this case, it must be impure hay," concluded Ricki. "But Salina hadn't had any hay for some time. It looked like she had been standing forever in the paddock, which didn't have any grass except for weeds."

"Ah, that's interesting. That means there are other possibilities," responded the vet.

"Like what?"

"Either the little pony ate some indigestible plant or she ate some grass roots; or perhaps she ate too many apples or pears. It's possible that there were fruit trees in the paddock. Ricki, I can't tell you what caused it, but now we have to try to get the digestive tract functioning again with a mild diet."

"How?"

"First I'm going to give her a shot so that the digestive tract calms down a bit. Give her the worm treatment tomorrow, because that's the most important thing for the digestion. And please, pay close attention that she isn't overfed, and especially that Salina doesn't eat Chico's rations. It's probably best to tie the two of them up when they're being fed so that the pony eats only her food! After two or three days, make her some oatmeal once a day so that the stomach and the intestines can calm down. Make sure that the oatmeal is tepid, not any warmer, when you feed her, otherwise the result will be the opposite of what we want."

Ricki nodded. "Okay, I'll do it. When will you be back to check on her?" she asked.

"I think, if nothing extraordinary happens, it would be enough if I examine her in a week." The vet patted Ricki on the shoulder encouragingly. "Don't worry, we'll fix her up as good as new."

Dr. Hofer prepared the injection he had just mentioned. While he injected the medicine into Salina's neck muscle, the little mare stood as still as a statue. She seemed to sense that these people wanted to help her, and she was very grateful to them.

"See you in a week, Ricki. Take care. And if anything happens, just give me a call, okay?"

"Sure! Bye, Doctor Hofer, and thanks for everything," she said as she accompanied the vet to the door.

"See you," he called back as he hurried to his car. His next four-legged patient was already waiting for him.

*

Cathy and Kevin sat across from each other in the ice cream shop drinking strawberry milkshakes.

Kevin held his head in his hands and stared at his drink. Cathy felt really sorry for him, but she found it hard to express herself. She couldn't rid herself of the idea that anything she said to him would be the wrong thing.

*

After leaving the stall in such a hurry the day before, Kevin had gone straight home and locked himself in his room. He wanted to avoid any conversation with Carlotta. His mother – who was Carlotta's housekeeper and lived with Kevin in a separate apartment in Carlotta's large house –

had raised her eyebrows in astonishment when her son came home from the stable so early in the afternoon.

"What's going on?" she asked politely as he rushed through the door.

"Nothing!" Kevin pushed past her without another word.

"Are you sure?"

"Yes!"

"Would you like a piece of cake? I baked a marble –"

"No!" Annoyed, the boy disappeared inside his room and slammed the door loudly.

Puzzled, Caroline Thomas watched him go.

"Well, thanks for the pleasant conversation," she announced. She shook her head and went back into the kitchen.

*

Now Cathy sat across from Kevin in the ice cream shop and hoped that he would begin to talk. After all, they had agreed to come here so they could talk.

"Are all girls like that? Do they just dump their boyfriends when someone else comes along?" Kevin asked suddenly. He looked right at Cathy.

You broke up with her, Cathy thought to herself.

"No, I don't think so!" she answered instead. "I don't think I would. If I cared for someone, then I wouldn't even look at anyone else."

"Are you sure of that?" asked Kevin, with interest.

Cathy nodded vigorously. "I'm pretty sure!"

"Do you think Ricki is really in love with that Lex? Or could it be that I'm just imagining things? Lillian said something like that."

Cathy sensed how difficult it had been for Kevin to say these words. If she were honest with herself, she'd have to admit that he was imagining a lot more – as far as Ricki and Lex were concerned – than had actually happened.

Since she had rediscovered her suppressed feelings for Kevin, she saw her chance to separate Ricki and him once and for all. Maybe someday she could become Kevin's girlfriend.

"I don't want to hurt you," said Cathy softly, "but you saw yourself how she looked at him."

"Hmm." Kevin returned to complete silence while observing Cathy closely. He was really grateful that she was sitting with him and helping him to sort through his feelings.

"I'm glad you're here," he said after a few minutes. He smiled at Cathy with deeply sad eyes. Then he put his hand on hers.

Cathy swallowed. In this moment she felt really ashamed of herself, but she would probably never have another chance like this to win Kevin over. She pressed his hand back.

"It's okay," she replied with a shaky voice. "I'm happy to be here with you. You're a great guy, Kevin!"

Kevin's eyes filled with tears, but he wasn't embarrassed that Cathy saw them.

He felt so alone, so betrayed, so – He couldn't even begin to describe how he felt.

"Darn!" he said tonelessly, before letting go of the girl's hand and turning his head away abruptly.

Cathy's heart was heavy. It hurt her to see Kevin suffering so much. She spontaneously got up, went around the table, and put her arms around his neck.

"You want to leave?" she asked gently. The boy nodded. "Come on, then. I'll walk you home."

Cathy took his arm and they left the ice cream shop quickly, leaving the other teenagers in the shop wondering what was going on between them.

Chapter 6

"Well, Ricki, everything okay?" Marcus Sulai asked his daughter as he turned the corner of the stable. "How's our four-legged guest?"

"Pretty good, I think," Ricki smiled at her father. "We brought them all out onto the paddock a little while ago. The vet thought it would be okay."

"Great!" Ricki's father looked around, searching for Ricki's friends. "Are you all alone today? Where are the others?"

"I have no idea," Ricki answered as nonchalantly as she could.

"They're having a fight!" Harry announced loudly.

"That's not true!" his sister yelled at him.

"Yes it is! I heard you!"

"Oh, shut up!"

"Ricki, please don't take that tone with your brother."

The girl rolled her eyes and tried to get away quickly, but Marcus held her back.

"Listen, we're going into town with Jake. He has an appointment with the doctor and we're going to do some shopping while he's there. We may be gone quite a while."

"Okay. See you."

"Yeah, see you," repeated Marcus, looking thoughtfully at his daughter as she disappeared quickly into the stable. But then he just shrugged his shoulders and pushed Harry toward the car, where Jake and Brigitte were already waiting.

When Ricki noticed that the sound of the motor was becoming fainter, she breathed a sigh of relief. Great! She wouldn't be bothered by anyone for at least two or three hours.

What? TWO or THREE hours? Ricki collapsed in a heap. What would she do if her friends didn't come to the farm?

Lillian is the only friend I have left anyway, Ricki realized sadly. Lost in thought, she walked down the path to the paddock to sit down in the shade of a linden tree.

Diablo, who saw her immediately, came trotting over to her. Salina accompanied him.

"You guys are my friends, anyway," the girl murmured. She stroked their beautiful heads, one after the other, as they bent trustingly toward her.

"This evening, I'm going to make the two of you even more beautiful," Ricki promised them before they went back to grazing.

Salina seemed contented. The other animals had accepted her and – even though her belly still looked like a barrel – she wasn't in pain, plus she was enjoying the sunny day and the fact that she was no longer alone.

Ricki leaned back and closed her eyes.

She still felt exhausted after the sleepless night, and gradually her sleepiness began to overtake her. The idyllic quiet all around her did the rest. In a few minutes, Ricki fell asleep.

*

She was having a beautiful dream in which she was walking hand in hand with Kevin around Echo Lake. But what was going on? Into her dream came Lex, who took her in his arms – while smiling happily – and in the distance she saw Kevin on Charon, galloping away from her.

Ricki became restless. She heard a whinny from somewhere, but she wasn't sure if the sound was in her dream or –

Suddenly she opened her eyes, confused. She looked all around.

Diablo stood next to her, scraping the ground excitedly with his front hoof.

"Hey, what's going on?" Ricki wasn't completely awake when she caught a glimpse of Sharazan, who was lying in the middle of the paddock. He was turning his head back and forth while kicking his belly with his hind legs.

"Oh, no!" With one huge jump, Ricki was up and running toward the roan. "Sharazan, what's wrong with you? Come on, get up!"

The girl made gestures with her arms as she ran. She shouted at the horse, but instead of reacting normally and getting up, the horse remained on the ground.

When Ricki – frightened and nervous – reached Sharazan, she observed his legs. Her first thought was that the horse might have stumbled and fallen, spraining one of his pastern joints. But she couldn't find any indication of swelling.

With a shaky voice, Ricki spoke to Kevin's horse. She tried to get closer, but Sharazan kicked uncontrollably and bared his teeth. Ricki decided to play if safe and keep some distance between them.

Diablo, Holli, Rashid, and Salina stood like statues, watching their stablemate with questioning eyes. Chico trustingly walked toward Sharazan to get a closer look.

"Chico, no! Keep away!" Ricki bit her bottom lip. "Chico!"

It happened that fast!

Painfully struck by one of Sharazan's kicking legs, the donkey screamed and limped out of the danger zone.

"Oh, great!" mumbled Ricki. She hoped that the other animals would now stay away from Sharazan.

What was wrong with Sharazan, anyway? He had been just fine only minutes ago before she fell asleep.

What should I do? Ricki desperately wondered. Then she noticed that the roan's belly was swollen like a balloon.

The girl slapped her forehead. "Of course, colic! I should have thought of that from the beginning! Darn it, what now? If only Jake were here."

Ricki had never before been in a situation where she had to administer first aid to a horse with colic. All she knew was that she had to do whatever it took to get the horse to stand up and then she had to walk the horse. Under no circumstances could Sharazan remain lying on the ground!

Ricki's brain was working overtime. She knew that she would never be able to get Sharazan up on his feet by herself.

"The vet! I have to get the vet to come!" she said to herself. She turned abruptly and ran back to the house as fast as she could.

She dialed the vet's number – her hands trembling – and then ran over to the window with the receiver in her hand. She could see Sharazan still lying on the ground in the middle of the paddock.

"Come on, come on! Answer the phone, please!"

She hung up hastily and tried again, but now there was something wrong with the connection. All she heard was beeping and crackling noises.

Ricki tried five more times to reach Dr. Hofer, but it was in vain. Desperately, she slammed the receiver onto the cradle.

KEVIN! She had to reach Kevin or – even better – Carlotta, who was sure to know what to do. But when she tried to call them their lines were busy.

What do they have to talk about for so long, for heaven's sake? If I don't get some help soon, Sharazan could die, thought Ricki.

Then she thought of Lex. "But I don't even know his last name," she realized.

She went back to the window and observed Sharazan. It made her feel sick to see him in that condition. Diablo and the others were still not moving and were watching Kevin's horse. They sensed that something was wrong with him and that scared them.

Maybe Diablo could get Sharazan to stand up, thought

Ricki, but then she remembered Chico, who had been kicked. She dismissed that idea quickly.

I have to go back there, Ricki said to herself. She'd much rather have just disappeared into thin air, but instead she gathered all her courage and ran toward the paddock. As she approached the fence, she heard a loud car horn and saw a little beat-up old car coming toward her. Then she recognized Lex behind the wheel.

Ricki sent a silent prayer of thanks toward heaven as Lex brought his vehicle to a standstill and got out.

"Isn't this a beautiful day?" he shouted, beaming. "Your arm looks better –"

"Lex, I'm so glad you're here! Sharazan is lying back there on the meadow and I think he has colic! I can't get near him and I have no idea how to get him back up on his feet. I couldn't reach the vet, and –"

Before Ricki had stopped talking, Lex had crawled under the fence poles and begun to run toward Kevin's horse, past Diablo, who was spooked and galloping away.

Over the years, Lex had seen his father help a lot of colicky horses. So one look was all it took to tell him that Sharazan's condition was critical. They had to get the horse on his feet immediately before it was too late.

Sharazan was sweating profusely. The arteries in his head stood out, and the whites of his eyes were visible. Sharazan was obviously suffering terribly.

"A rope, Ricki! We need a long rope or a lunge line – quickly! And bring Diablo's snaffle, too!" he shouted at the girl. She only hesitated for a moment before running off to do as he asked.

"Hurry, we don't have much time left!" Lex's words echoed behind her.

Not much time left ... not much time ... The words hammered inside her skull. She was running so hard, she could barely breathe.

She stumbled into the stable, completely drained, and almost collapsed inside the tack room.

What did Lex say? A long rope? Where could she find a long rope around here? *Oh yeah, the lunge line, right*, and what else was she supposed to take along?

Ricki's thoughts were swirling through her head. She gazed restlessly back and forth around the tack room before she finally remembered Diablo's snaffle. She grabbed the things that Lex had wanted her to bring, took a deep breath, and ran back to the paddock.

Lex was waving impatiently and had come toward her a few yards.

"It looks bad. We really have to hurry," he urged and tore the lunge line out of Ricki's hands.

"Put Diablo's snaffle on – fast – and then come over here to Sharazan!" Lex gave abrupt orders and then just left the girl standing there.

"What's your plan?" asked Ricki, curious, but she knew that she couldn't expect any answers from Lex at the moment.

*

Randall, Pepe, Gringo, and a few others in the Western club had arrived back at the clearing to collect the outdoor furniture and some other stuff left behind after yesterday's party.

Even Lillian had volunteered to help, and Josh realized that the work was much more fun when his girlfriend was there with him.

"It's really great of you to help us," a pleasant young woman named Claudia said. They had just loaded a picnic table and benches onto the back of a pickup truck together.

"Have you been going with Josh long?" Claudia asked. She wiped her forehead, which was wet with perspiration from all the work.

Lillian nodded. "With Josh? Hmm, wait a minute ... no, we haven't been together very long."

Claudia laughed. "Well, that answers my question exactly."

"Hey, were you here yesterday? I didn't see you," said Lillian. "But that could be because I didn't stay at the party very long," she added.

"Oh no, I was busy yesterday. I heard it was a really great party. Unfortunately, I had to study," she added.

"Study? What are you studying, if I may ask?" Lillian looked at her questioningly.

"I'm studying to be a veterinarian – I'm in the pre-vet program at the college – and we had an exam this morning. You have to decide what's more important, good grades or a party. I thought, there'll be lots of parties, but if I fail the test, then –"

Lillian grinned; she was thinking about Lex.

"Yeah, I understand. It looks like we're going to have a lot of vets around here someday."

Claudia hesitated. "What do you mean by that?"

"Oh, nothing. Was that all of the picnic benches or are there more behind the cabin?" asked Lillian.

Claudia shrugged her shoulders. "No idea. Probably best to go and have a look, but let's grab a soda first, okay? It's really hot today."

Lillian gave her the thumbs up. "Good idea!" she said and smiled at Josh, who was rolling one of the barrels from the training area over to the pickup.

"Everything okay, you two? Are you taking a break already?" he called. Lillian just smiled and turned around.

"What do you mean, 'already'?" Claudia shot back. She took Lillian's arm and the two girls walked over to the cabin to see if they could find something cold to drink.

*

Hiram Parker was having one of his lucid moments, when he could think clearly about everything that was happening in his life. Most of the time, though, he seemed to be lost in another world.

"That's typical for Alzheimer's," the doctor said when the nurse reported her conversation with the old man to him.

"He's worried about his pony because there's no one at his farm to take care of it," she said. "And he said something about a will, which he left with his lawyers in case anything happened to him."

"Write down everything on his medical chart," the doctor advised. "After all, it's possible that he's never told anyone else about this. In addition, try to find out what happened to the pony after they brought him here."

93

"Is that part of my job as a nurse?" the young woman asked a little grumpily.

The doctor took a deep breath. "If you find out that the animal is being well taken care of, and you are able to relieve the old gentleman of one of his worries so that he has the time to get well, then yes, my dear, that's part of your job description. By the way, we don't work at 'jobs.' Ours is a profession."

The nurse's face turned bright red. She was embarrassed and left the room quickly.

I hope Mr. Parker finds out in time how his pony is doing, the doctor thought. The old man's condition was very serious.

*

"You're very different from Ricki," announced Kevin as he walked home beside Cathy.

"No two people are the same," the girl answered.

Cathy pretended to have trouble walking straight and kept bumping into the boy. "I feel a little dizzy today," she lied.

Kevin took her arm immediately. "Why didn't you tell me right away?"

Cathy was enjoying Kevin's company enormously. "So, are we going over to the stable today?" she asked.

Kevin made a face. "I don't know. To be honest, I don't feel like running into Ricki. I have to get over the thing with Lex first."

Cathy's heart soared. "But Sharazan and Rashid aren't to blame for your having broken up with Ricki," she said.

94

"You can go. After all, the thing between Ricki and me has nothing to do with you!" answered Kevin, annoyed.

"Maybe it does," Cathy said mysteriously.

Kevin stood still. "Why?" he wanted to know, amazed. Cathy remained silent, staring at him.

"Tell me," urged the boy. He tried to find an answer to his question in Cathy's expression.

A few seconds went by, and then a realization came to him.

"Oh, now I get it. You've got a crush on Lex, too!"

Cathy shook her head and felt her face turn red.

"No, Kevin, not on Lex –" she whispered. She tore herself away and ran off.

Bewildered, the boy watched her go.

Did she just tell me that she's got a crush on me? he asked himself, shaking his head, while watching Cathy in the distance. *Well, I'll have to think about that for a bit. She's really nice, and a good pal, but ... I think I'm in a bit of a mess, after everything I've said to her.*

Slowly, Kevin started walking again. He was very glad when he finally arrived home.

There were too many thoughts running through his head and he had the feeling that he didn't understand anything anymore. He had to talk with someone about it, someone who wasn't in any way involved.

Carlotta. I think I'll talk with Carlotta. She always knows what to do, he thought.

*

Lex had run around Sharazan and was now behind the horse's back, where he didn't have to worry about being kicked.

Slowly, gradually, he got closer. He began speaking to the horse quietly, but Sharazan didn't react to his words at all. Just as before, Sharazan's eyes looked panic-stricken. Lex realized that Kevin's horse was having more and more difficulty breathing.

"It's okaaay." Lex tried to calm down the animal, while he got closer and closer to Sharazan, the lunge line with the snap hook held tightly in his hand.

*

Ricki needed several minutes to catch Diablo, who was nervous, but she had finally succeeded in pulling the snaffle over his head and was just about to buckle the leather straps in place.

"Stand still, darn it!" she shouted, exasperated at her horse, who kept trying to shake off the harness.

Finally, Ricki succeeded. She looked over at Lex, still wondering what he was planning and why she'd had to harness Diablo.

Lex was standing near the withers of the horse and staring at Sharazan. The horse – obviously in a great deal of pain – kept thrashing his head back and forth on the ground.

Lex stood there and waited for the right moment. Then, just when Sharazan's head remained on the ground for a second, he jumped forward.

With one motion, he was beside Sharazan. He put his knee on the horse's neck to keep him still so that he could snap the lunge line onto the halter.

Immediately afterward, Lex jumped out of the horse's range.

"Ricki, bring Diablo over here! Quick!" he shouted, waving excitedly to the girl.

Ricki had a little trouble getting Diablo to move to within six feet of Sharazan, but finally she managed.

Lex quickly put one end of the lunge line around Diablo's neck. He tied a knot so that it couldn't slip and become any tighter. Then he grabbed Diablo's reins and began to pull.

"Come, Diablo. Come on. Forward," he called.

Lex hoped that Diablo would be able to get Kevin's horse to stand up by using his pulling strength, but at first it looked like their efforts weren't succeeding.

Ricki had stepped to the side so that she wouldn't be in the way. From there she cheered her horse on.

"Come on, Diablo. Let's go. Come on! Pull, my boy. Pull, Diablo, PULL!"

Ricki's black horse walked forward, but as soon as he felt the resistance of Sharazan's weight, he stopped and stood still, perplexed. A horse that had been used to pulling a wagon probably wouldn't have thought anything about it, but this was a completely new situation for Diablo.

Upset, he snorted through his nostrils, looking accusingly at Lex.

"Now come on, come ... come ... come!" ordered Lex sharply, but it was impossible to get Diablo to move even three feet forward. Behind him, Sharazan had become terribly quiet.

Lex threw a worried glance at Kevin's horse, while Ricki wanted to shout out her frustration and fear.

"Okay, then we'll do it differently!" Lex threw Diablo's reins over his neck, grabbed hold of the long mane, and swung himself up onto the horse's bare back.

He sat up quickly and pressed his legs tightly against Diablo's belly.

Ricki's horse jerked, then hesitated for a split second before he followed Lex's energetic signal. Diablo began walking forward, step by step. The lunge line lay like an iron strap around his muscular neck.

Diablo didn't like the feeling at all and whinnied pleadingly, but Lex forced him forward while looking back at Sharazan, who stretched out his neck with a tortured look in his eyes. Ricki was afraid that the harness would tear.

"Ricki, get out of the way!" yelled Lex as he noticed that Ricki had run back to Sharazan and was standing beside the horse, who was now lying on his stomach.

"Get away!" yelled Lex again, but Ricki just ignored him. She was observing Diablo closely, and as he pulled again, she screamed shrilly – as loud as she could – and then she slapped the roan on the croup with her open hand.

Even though the pain was terrible, Kevin's gelding was terribly frightened. He pulled himself upright with the last ounce of strength left in him, to get away from this screaming and any more slaps.

"Thank God," exploded Lex. His joy wasn't just over the

fact that the horse was finally standing up. He was glad that nothing had happened to Ricki.

Lex didn't give Sharazan any time to lie down again. He quickly bent down to the lunge line and rolled it up quite a way before pulling Sharazan after him, while he rode Diablo all over the paddock.

Well, we managed this part, but what now? he thought to himself.

Then suddenly it came to him. "That's it! Ricki, run over to my car. There's a little box in the trunk with all kinds of things in it. There should be a green-and-white package with little plastic bottles. Please bring me one of those bottles quickly. They're about four inches tall and filled with a brown fluid. Hurry!" he called to the girl, as he continued to ride Diablo and pull Sharazan behind him.

Ricki ran across the paddock. As she crawled under the fence poles, she banged her head painfully.

"That's all I need!" she groaned and kept going.

She found the bottles quickly and was on her way back to the paddock.

"Here," she called from a distance and held the bottle out to Lex.

He jumped down from Diablo's back.

"Open it!" he ordered, as he grabbed Sharazan's halter tightly. "So, you got it?"

Ricki was desperate. "I can't get the stupid thing open! Is there some trick to it?"

"You have to twist the top and break it off at the same time!"

Finally, she got it off and relieved, held it out to Lex.

99

"Help me hold Sharazan," ordered Lex. Ricki tightened her grip around the halter, and then the young man took the bottle and pressed it on the place in the horse's mouth where there are no teeth. He made sure that the fluid ran over Sharazan's tongue.

Kevin's horse rolled his eyes nervously, and tried with all his might to get away from the two people who seemed to be torturing him. Although Ricki had to let go pretty quickly, Lex held on.

Sharazan's tongue began to burn. He tried to spit out the horrible stuff, but Lex had already counted on that reaction.

Using all his strength, he pressed the horse's head upward and held it in that position until the horse had swallowed. Only then was Sharazan allowed to let his head sink downward.

"What is that stuff?" asked Ricki, who was sniffing the empty bottle and making a face.

"Among other things, there is aniseed, fennel, and caraway oil in it, and they have a positive effect on fermentation and cramps in the digestive tract. It's sort of first aid for colic, diarrhea, and similar problems. We have to give Sharazan some tepid warm water afterward. That stuff makes you thirsty," explained Lex. "I had almost forgotten that I still had that stuff in the car. Actually, it was for Pepe's horse. But we've got to keep him moving! He can't stand still, otherwise all this effort will have been for nothing!"

Lex rode around and around, while Ricki freed Diablo from the lunge line and took off his snaffle.

"I'm going to try to reach the vet again," she called to Lex as she ran back to the house.

100

"Dear God, please let Sharazan live and let me reach Doctor Hofer," prayed Ricki over and over again. A little later the heavens seemed, once again, to be answering her prayers. After three rings, Ricki finally had the vet on the line.

Chapter 7

Cathy had run home and retreated into her room with a glass of orange juice and a full box of chocolate-chip cookies. She wasn't so sure – now that she'd had time to think about it – that it had been a good idea to give Kevin the impression that she had a crush on him.

Nervously, she stuffed one cookie after another into her mouth while she gave some thought to what her next move should be.

She got up and stood in front of the large mirror that was attached to her closet door. She examined herself critically, from top to bottom, turning from side to side. "Darn it, I'm way too fat!" she realized in frustration. She was forced to think about Ricki, who had always had a good figure and of whom she had always been secretly jealous. Furious, she threw a half-eaten cookie back into the box and crossed her arms in front of her chest.

I have to lose weight! she thought. She knew that Kevin liked thin girls. She'd heard him say so.

The image in the mirror stared back at her grimly. Cathy

wanted to throw something at it, but that wouldn't help her shed one pound and she knew it.

Ricki has everything I want, she thought with a new wave of envy. *She has her own horse, her own stable, a good figure, and she's popular with everyone. She doesn't have Kevin anymore, but whether he wants to be with me is another question entirely. Life is so unfair!*

At least, Cathy remembered, there's one thing that doesn't belong to Ricki. That was Rashid, who meant everything to Cathy.

She sighed. What a shame that Rashid was boarding at the Sulais' stable. There was no way she could spend any time with her foster horse without running into Ricki. Suddenly Cathy felt a little guilty, even though her friend had no idea about her feelings for Kevin.

"Oh, why should I feel guilty?" she mumbled to herself. "After all, Ricki did this to herself. If she hadn't flirted so much with Lex, everything would be like it always was. And as far as my feelings for Kevin are concerned," she told herself, returning her gaze to the mirror, "I can't just ignore them ... can I?"

Determined, she walked to the door. She would ride her bike to the stables. She was sure that Rashid was waiting for her – as he always was every day – and that he would be glad to see her. Maybe Lillian would be there too, and they could go riding together.

*

Kevin had a long conversation with Carlotta, who listened attentively to everything he said. She then carefully tried to explain to him that jealousy – especially when it was without any proof – could destroy everything.

Kevin swallowed hard. "But what should I do, then? Ricki's flirting with Lex really hurt me."

Carlotta, sensing the boy was trying to justify his feelings, just shook her head. "Flirting can be exciting and great fun, but it has nothing at all to do with real love," she explained convincingly. "And don't tell me that since you've been seeing Ricki, you've never had the urge to flirt with a pretty girl."

"No!"

Carlotta had to smile. "What about Melanie? Remember? Josh's pretty young cousin? That was only a few months ago."

Kevin turned red. He did remember. To his surprise, he'd quickly become interested in the girl, to the point where it almost ruined his relationship with Ricki.

"That ... that was something entirely different." He was trying to squirm out of this jam, but Carlotta wasn't about to let him.

"No, no, my boy. The only difference is that then it was Ricki who suffered because of your flirtation with Melanie. Think about it, Kevin, and make sure you know what your real feelings are. Think about what Ricki means to you and whether you might have overreacted a bit in the situation with Lex. I'm sure that Ricki was more interested in the horse than in that young man, and if it's about horses, well, actually, you, as a rider, should be more understanding about that, shouldn't you?"

Kevin nodded and left the room feeling remorseful and embarrassed.

If Carlotta is right, then I'm the biggest jerk in the world, he thought. And he wondered if Ricki would be open to at least talking with him. He didn't want to end the close relationship they had.

I'll go over to the stable, he decided impulsively. *Hopefully, Ricki will be home, and, hopefully, she'll be willing to talk. I don't want to lose her!*

He ran down the stairs and slammed the front door behind him. Then he jumped on his bike and pedaled away furiously.

Carlotta stood at the window on the second floor with the curtains pushed to one side. She had observed Kevin leaving, and she smiled and nodded encouragingly.

It would be a pity if those two weren't able to get through this, she thought, as she watched the boy ride away until he disappeared around the next street corner.

*

Dr. Hofer had driven to the Sulai farm as fast as his car could go. According to Ricki's description, he couldn't afford to lose any time treating Sharazan. Now the vet stood on the paddock where Lex had tirelessly led Kevin's horse around. He had a very concerned look on his face.

After giving the horse a thorough examination, the vet opened his bag and prepared two injections while Lex explained to him that he had already given Sharazan a natural herbal remedy. Ricki had removed the instructions from the package from Lex's car and was holding them in front of Dr. Hofer's face. The vet looked over the list of ingredients and then nodded in agreement and recognition.

"That was exactly right," he said seriously. "You probably saved Sharazan's life with that medicine!"

Ricki and Lex both breathed sighs of relief as the vet began to give the horse the injections. Sharazan had calmed down somewhat in the meantime.

"Have you ever thought about becoming a vet?" asked Dr. Hofer.

Lex had to laugh. "I'm doing what I can, but I still need a few more years!" he grinned at Dr. Hofer.

The vet grinned back at him but then he got serious again. "I thought we'd have to give Sharazan an infusion, but it looks as though we won't have to after all. The best thing would be to lead him around for another half hour and then bring him back to his stall. Tie him up so that he doesn't eat any straw before this evening, but make sure that he has enough to drink. That's really important. Also, he will probably sweat quite a bit. Do you have blankets to absorb the perspiration?"

Ricki nodded.

"Good, then put one on him now. However, as soon as it's damp, you'll have to change the blanket. This could take a few hours, but you'll have to get through it."

Dr. Hofer patted Sharazan's neck affectionately. "Later I'll look in on the donkey. I think he's okay, but I'll be back this evening to make sure. Let me give you my cell phone number just in case. You can reach me any time with that, if there are any complications. Does Kevin know how lucky he is?"

"No," answered Ricki as she accompanied the vet back to his car while Lex began to lead Sharazan around in circles again. "I tried to call him but his phone was always busy!"

Dr. Hofer gave the girl a business card with three different phone numbers on it.

"Well, that young man will be grateful to you two for the rest of his life," he said with a wink. Then he glanced once more at Sharazan. "It could have ended really badly if you two hadn't done what you did in time. Well, I'll see you later, Ricki. Say hi to Jake for me. Where is he, anyway?"

"At the doctor."

"Oh, I wondered where he was. I hope he's all right." Dr. Hofer started his car and drove off in the direction of the main road.

*

A half hour later, Ricki opened the gate to the paddock for Lex and Sharazan. Together, they brought the animal back to the stable.

The roan was perfectly content to trot beside them, and – in comparison to his earlier, colicky behavior, when he had been in a frenzy – he now gave the impression that he was coming out of it.

After Lex had tied Sharazan up securely, Ricki put the blanket over him to absorb his sweat and placed a bucket of tepid water down on the ground within his reach. Then she left the stall and sat down beside Lex on a bale of straw in the corridor.

For a while, they sat silently, then suddenly Ricki asked, "Would you like something to drink?"

Lex nodded. "I'd love a cold soda."

"Good!" Ricki got up to go get the soda, but after a few steps, she came back and stood in front of Lex, who stared at her in surprise.

"Did I thank you yet for your help?" she asked him. She bent down and gave the bewildered young man a kiss on the cheek. "I'm sorry. I just had to do it," she laughed. As she turned around, she bumped into Kevin. He was completely incredulous over what he had just seen.

"Hey, Kevin. What are you doing here?" asked Ricki, surprised and a little embarrassed.

"Please, excuse me if I'm disturbing you two, but I happen to have a horse here," the boy answered coolly. He pushed Ricki aside in an attempt to get to Sharazan. "Just because you don't want anything more to do with me doesn't mean you should take it out on my horse," he added angrily. Carlotta had been wrong, and if Ricki was fooling around with Lex in the stalls, then it was clearly already a done deal.

"What do you mean by that?" asked Ricki, puzzled. "What do you think I would do to your horse?"

"All of the other horses are outside on the paddock. Sharazan's the only one who isn't! Do I have to look for another stable for him, just because I broke up with you? Isn't he even allowed to go outside?"

Ricki looked at Lex for some assistance. He had gotten up slowly, and now he was walking toward Kevin.

"I think, Kevin, that you have misunderstood a few things," he began in a calm voice. Kevin, however, stared at him with his eyes full of hatred.

"I think what I saw was pretty clear, don't you? Let me through. I want to bring my horse outside to the paddock."

"Sharazan had a colic, and Lex saved his life! Doctor Hofer has already been here, and –" Ricki burst out, but Kevin just looked at her with disgust.

"And the kiss was a thank-you kiss because he saved my horse? Oh, c'mon, Ricki, you can do better than that!" Kevin made a gesture with his finger on his forehead and tried to get past Lex, but Lex grabbed hold of his arm and forced Kevin to look at him.

"Let me go!" said Kevin, ominously calm, but Lex didn't let Kevin upset him.

"Look, you jealous idiot," he said, and pushed Kevin over to the bale of straw. "Sit down, here. Shut up for a few minutes and just listen!"

"Who do you think you are that you can tell me what I can and can't do?" yelled Kevin. "Just because you're a few years older, and –"

"KEVIN, that's enough!" Ricki had placed herself in front of Kevin, and was staring at him with her eyes blazing. "The only one who is making a scene is YOU! I don't even know who you are anymore! But that isn't really any of my concern any longer, is it? After all, you broke up with me yesterday! Even so, the least that you could have done would have been to tell me yourself, instead of sending Lillian! But whatever! You don't understand anything, not even the fact that Sharazan almost died today. I couldn't get anyone on the phone, and you can imagine how glad I was to see Lex, who just happened to come by. You should be grateful to him, because he was the one who managed to get Sharazan back up on his feet. He gave your horse a remedy for colic and walked him around in circles for hours so that he wouldn't lie down again. I think a thank-you kiss was appropriate because I had no idea what to do, and without him, well ... we might have lost Sharazan. So, do you get it now? Do you understand what happened here while you were sitting around feeling jealous and sorry for yourself? And now, Kevin, excuse me, but it's time to change Sharazan's sweaty blanket!" Ricki's voice began to tremble, so she turned around abruptly and raced over to the stall of the sick horse.

Kevin had turned pale and stared after Ricki, who was going over to Sharazan with a dry blanket.

"Sharazan –?" As though a wasp had stung him, Kevin jumped up suddenly and ran over to his horse.

Shaken, he leaned against the door to the stall and watched Ricki change Sharazan's blanket. His legs felt as though they were about to give out. Silently, he stared at his horse, who just stood there, his head hanging down, not even aware that his owner was there with him.

Ricki stroked the horse lovingly on the forehead before she gave Kevin a dirty look and left the stall to stand outside in the corridor.

"Helloooo, anyone home?" the sound came from outside the stable. Right afterward, Lillian and Josh came in, followed by an attractive young woman.

"Well, look who's here," the young woman said, laughing, when she caught sight of Lex. "So this is where you've been for the last few hours, while I've been waiting for you to pick me up! Did you forget that we had a date?"

110

Lex grinned. "No, but anything connected to my future career is simply more important! We might as well get used to that if we're going to be vets. Hello, Claudia, glad you're here." And he gave her a loving embrace.

Ricki felt a little hurt while witnessing this touching scene. But, she realized, she should have known that Lex would have a girlfriend his own age. If she were honest with herself, she had to admit that what she felt for Lex had really just been a crush. Her heart still belonged to Kevin.

"Ricki, let me introduce my girlfriend. This is Claudia. She's studying to be a vet, too, and we want to open a practice together someday," said Lex, beaming. Then Lex turned to Claudia, "And this is Ricki. I told you about her this morning on the phone."

"Hi, Ricki! Nice to meet you! Lillian and Josh just took me with them, when Lex stood me up –" Her glance fell through the open stall door onto Sharazan. "What's wrong with that horse?" she asked almost without a pause. This time Kevin had a chance to hear an even more detailed account of what had happened earlier.

Finally, the boy – who had already lost one beloved horse – understood what had occurred during his absence. In addition, after seeing Lex's girlfriend, he realized how idiotic and hurtful he had acted toward Ricki. He felt small and petty. If he could, he would have liked to crawl into a mouse hole and disappear.

I really am the biggest jerk of all time, he thought, hiding his face in Sharazan's mane.

Lillian poked Ricki and pointed at Kevin, but Ricki just

shrugged her shoulders before leaving the stable with the others.

"Don't forget to change the blanket when it gets damp," she called over her shoulder to Kevin.

"I bet his head is really going around in circles," Lillian laughed a little. Ricki, who really didn't find it that amusing, said a little sadly, "That's what he gets! After the way he's acted, he deserves to be upset for a while!"

"Absolutely!"

Lillian, Josh, and Ricki followed Lex and Claudia over to Lex's old car.

"What are you two going to do today?" Josh wanted to know as the couple got into the car.

"What do you think? Study!" Lex grinned and gave Claudia a kiss.

"Yeah, sure!" Josh teased. Lillian poked him playfully in the ribs.

Lex and Claudia waved as they drove off. Ricki was afraid that the car would break down. It rattled and chugged so much.

"Claudia seems really nice," she said to her girlfriend, who nodded in agreement.

"Yeah, she is. They make a really cute couple!"

That's true, Ricki admitted to herself. At that instant she realized how lonely she felt.

*

Josh had driven home, too. After he left, Lillian and Ricki decided to do Jake a favor and clean out the stalls for the evening. While Lillian dealt with the pitchfork, Ricki filled the hayracks.

Kevin had stationed himself in Sharazan's stall. The only time they saw him was when he brought the damp blankets outside to dry in the sun.

Ricki tried to ignore him, but she slowly realized that she was laughing way too often, way too loud, and way too fake.

Why am I doing this? she asked herself each time. She began to see that she wanted to show Kevin how happy she was without him. But the exact opposite was true.

*

"Your family has been gone for a long time," exclaimed Lillian when she was done sweeping.

"Hmm, maybe Jake had to wait a long time at the doctor's. Oh, well, at least we're done with the stalls! Want to get the animals from the paddock?"

"We can, but there are only two of us."

"Well, then we'll take Diablo and Holli first, and then we'll go back for Rashid, Chi –"

At that moment they heard someone clearing his throat. The sound was coming from Sharazan's stall. Embarrassed, Kevin came out.

"I can help you guys," he said softly, without looking at Ricki.

"Wow, are you still around?" Lillian took a deep breath to add something to her sentence, but Ricki shook her head silently.

"Okay, then let's go!" Lillian got the leads from the windowsill. Together but without speaking, the three of them walked down to the paddock. Their horses, plus Chico and Salina, were already waiting for them by the fence.

*

Cathy had taken many detours and had stopped to say hello to several classmates, because she just couldn't bring herself to ride her bike to the stable. Later in the day – when there was simply no one left for her to visit – she finally headed slowly toward the Sulai farm.

She saw the vet's car in the distance and assumed that Dr. Hofer had come by to check on Salina again.

"We were lucky this time," Cathy heard the vet say, as she entered the stable a short time later. When she saw Ricki, Lillian, and Kevin with Sharazan, she stopped short.

"What's going on?" she asked, as innocently as possible, and came so close that Kevin could feel her breath. He automatically moved back a little.

"He had colic," he told Cathy brusquely, before leading his horse back into the stall. Dr. Hofer had just finished his examination of Sharazan and had turned to leave.

Cathy felt a little unsure of herself. She decided to devote her attention to the care of Rashid.

While she was brushing him, she kept glancing cautiously at Kevin. He seemed to be trying to get close to Ricki.

"You've been brushing Rashid on the same spot for about ten minutes," announced Lillian. She had been watching Cathy. Caught in the act, the girl jumped, and then she asked, trying to appear as uninterested as possible, "Are those two getting along, again?"

Lillian raised her eyebrows. "And if they are? Is that a problem for you?"

Cathy pretended to be bored and shrugged her shoulders. "I don't care! I'm just asking!"

"Oh! Well, then –" Lillian walked over to Ricki. "Do you want me to groom Salina?"

"Oh, that would be great," came the reply from Diablo's stall. "I think by the time I'm finished with Diablo, my wrist will give out anyway!"

"If you want, I'll finish grooming him for you." Kevin had stepped behind Ricki.

"You?" The girl just looked at him.

Kevin nodded, embarrassed. "Ricki, I think we should talk," he said so softly that she was the only one who heard him.

"Why?" asked Ricki just as softly. "I thought there was nothing else to say?"

Kevin took a deep breath and then put his hand on Ricki's shoulder.

"Please, Ricki, I acted like such a moron, I ... c'mon, let's go outside for a minute," he pleaded. Sighing, Ricki gave in.

Together they left Diablo's stall. Then, hardly two minutes later, they left the stable. Cathy watched them with growing concern.

Quickly, she slipped out of Rashid's stall, but before she could follow the two of them, she heard Lillian's voice.

"Leave them alone, Cathy! They don't need anyone else around. They have things to say to each other."

"But I just wanted to –"

"I know what you wanted. I'm not stupid! Stay here, do you understand?!"

Cathy turned bright red. Had she allowed everyone else to see how she felt about Kevin?

Defeated, she shuffled back into Rashid's stall and began to unravel his tail with shaky fingers. As she did so, she listened closely, trying to hear something of what was being said. But Ricki and Kevin had walked several yards away, so that they could talk in private.

After what seemed to Cathy to be a very long time, they came back in together. They were holding hands and smiling again.

Ricki beamed liked she used to, and even Kevin seemed relieved.

"Hey, you guys, looks like there's a reason to celebrate," said Lillian, grinning across Salina's back.

"There is!" confirmed Ricki.

"Of course there is!" said Kevin. "Sharazan is alive, Salina's doing well, and I have my girlfriend back. If those aren't reasons to celebrate, then I don't know what are!" Happy, he lifted Ricki off the floor and danced her around in circles.

Lillian laughed. "Well, then, congratulations on your new, old relationship!" she said heartily. She looked over at Cathy, who could hardly keep the tears back.

Ricki, who had heard from Kevin about his conversations with Cathy, had noticed the changes in her and could even understand her feelings. Ricki pulled away from Kevin and walked over to Rashid's stall.

"Cathy," she began slowly, "I think I know how you feel, and I also know how much you like Kevin. I can imagine that you're disappointed that we are back together, but I'm positive that you'll find someone soon, too. And then you'll understand, why we're ... well, why Kevin and I are back together."

Cathy stared at Ricki. She could hardly believe what she had just heard.

Obviously, Ricki wasn't mad at her at all, and that made Cathy uneasy. Especially, when she thought of how envious she had been of Ricki in the last few days.

"I think it's better for me to go back home," Cathy began, stumbling over her words. She tried to get past Ricki.

"Don't be weird, Cathy," responded Kevin. "I think both of us were pretty unfair, and a lot of what was said was misinterpreted. Maybe we should just forget the whole thing."

"Good idea," agreed Lillian, and then clapped Kevin on the shoulder, laughing. "So, we were never at Josh's party, Salina doesn't exist for us, Ricki's wrist is fine, we never met Lex and Claudia, you never broke up with Ricki, and therefore, Cathy has no reason to feel upset!"

"Exactly!" exclaimed Ricki. "And do you know what the best part of it is? Sharazan won't have had colic and will be standing in his stall in great shape! But if we forget everything, we won't have any reason to celebrate."

"Oh, we'll think of something. Is it anyone's birthday or anything?" asked Lillian. She was in a good mood and noticed that even Rashid's remorseful caretaker was smiling a little.

"Well, I think I know something we could celebrate," said Cathy quietly.

"Tell us!"

"There's a Children's Day, Mothers' Day, Fathers' Day, but is there a Friends' Day?"

"Cathy, that's a great idea! I have no idea if there is such a holiday, but I am definitely in favor of starting this holiday, at least for us," called Ricki enthusiastically. She was so glad that she and Kevin were back together, and she latched onto Cathy's suggestion immediately, because she didn't want to lose that friendship either.

"Therefore, I designate this day as Friends' Day, to be celebrated annually," Ricki announced ceremoniously. Then she ran over to the house to get some soda, pretzels, and potato chips from her mother's stash. The four friends had a picnic right there in the stable. They kept looking at Sharazan the whole time, but the horse's temperature happily seemed to have gone back to normal.

When Jake finally arrived at the stable an hour later, he found the friends having a great time together.

"Well, that was really a horrible day," he said. "First, there were ten people ahead of me in the waiting room, and then, when it was finally my turn, the doctor was called away to an emergency and he didn't get back for an hour! Your parents, Ricki, were shopping. They had to wait for me for a long time, and just when we were about to drive home, your father noticed that the car had a flat tire. We had to go to a garage because the spare tire was flat, too." Jake groaned. "Everything okay with you guys? My heavens, I wish my life was as easy as yours."

118

"Well, Jake, Sharazan had a serious colic attack, but otherwise, we're fine," said Ricki, as she munched on a handful of potato chips.

"WHAT?" yelped Jake, but he calmed down when he saw that Kevin's horse was already chewing on some hay. "Well, that's just typical," he said. "I can't even leave you alone for half a day without something happening!"

"Everything's fine again, Jake," replied Ricki. She tried to downplay the fear she'd had when Sharazan had been so ill with colic. In addition, she didn't want the old man to get too upset. "Doctor Hofer – with Lex's assistance – got everything under control. Lillian and I cleaned out the stalls. So your work is done for today."

Jake shook his head. "That's just like you! You young people don't take things seriously enough," he scolded before he left the stable to get changed.

He has no idea, thought Ricki to herself, and then she leaned back happily against Kevin.

119

Chapter 8

Over the next few days, the young friends returned to their normal routines, except that Kevin didn't take part in the daily rides so that Sharazan could recuperate.

Everyone was relieved to see that Salina was responding to the care she was receiving at the Sulais'. Her distended belly was shrinking to a normal size, and she was grazing and playing contentedly with the other animals, who had accepted her into their "family."

Ricki and Kevin had resolved their differences. Peace and harmony had returned to the foursome, which only a few days before been in danger of losing some of its members.

Ricki and Kevin decided not to keep rehashing the whole misunderstanding with Lex, while Cathy tried to keep her jealousy under control. She'd come to realize that her friendship with Ricki, Kevin, and Lillian was more important to her than her petty, personal feelings.

*

A little more than a week after Ricki had brought Salina home with her, the police officer who'd questioned her about Hiram Parker drove up to the house.

Ricki, along with her parents and Carlotta, was standing in front of the house and talking. She was trying to get her parents' permission to spend the night in the stable with her friends, or at least to camp out in a tent behind the house. However, a resounding "NO!" from Ricki's mother made even the policeman jump. He quickly saw that he'd come in the middle of a family dispute. *They're always sticky*, he thought to himself. *When parents discuss things with their teenagers, it's always best to keep a distance.* He'd learned this from experience.

"Hello, everybody. I don't want to take up much of your time," he said, greeting them quickly.

"Oh, Officer – I'm sorry, I'm afraid I've forgotten your name," began Brigitte Sulai.

"Stevenson. Paul Stevenson."

"Officer Stevenson ... right. What brings you out here?"

The officer hesitated a bit and then turned to Ricki.

"Well, actually, there are two reasons. First –" he opened a plastic bag and held it in front of the girl – "I assume this belongs to you."

Puzzled, Ricki looked inside the bag. "Oh yes, the Western clothes. I'd completely forgotten about them. Thanks a lot for bringing them to me. They were borrowed," she said, feeling a little guilty.

"Good," the officer nodded. "That was easy. The next matter is a little more complicated. It's about Salina."

Ricki turned pale. "Has Mr. Parker been discharged from

121

the hospital? Does he want her back?" she asked, upset. She'd completely forgotten that Salina didn't belong to her.

"Oh, that's great," Brigitte joined in. "I'm sure he'll be happy to see that his pony is in good condition."

Ricki gave her father pleading looks to signal him that she was counting on his help. In the past week, as Marcus had watched his daughter care for the little pony, he'd come to understand how much Salina meant to her. *My kid*, he thought to himself with inner pride, *has got a heart full of love for that little animal, and for all animals*.

"Well," the officer began hesitantly, "I'm sorry to say that Mr. Parker died last night of a lung embolism."

"Oh," was the only thing Brigitte could say. But Ricki – too distraught to speak – swallowed hard. This was the first time she'd come in direct contact with death. All the images raced through her head – how she'd found the old man lying on the floor; how he had been placed into the ambulance. And she would never forget his cries to Salina.

"What will become of Salina?" she asked in a shaky voice. She glanced again at her father, fearfully.

"Well, Mr. Parker has no living relatives and apparently no friends. He lived alone. My task is to ask you if it would be possible for you to keep the animal, or if we should contact the animal shelter and have them pick her up. You were nice enough to say that you would be willing to keep her until her real owner was discharged from the hospital. So I just thought I'd ask."

"Please, Dad, I want Salina to stay here. She's gotten used to being here and has made friends with the other animals. We can't just let them take her away," Ricki pleaded.

She got really upset when her mother told the officer, "I'm sorry, Officer Stevenson, you don't know my daughter. If this pony stays here, it won't be long before she drags in another ailing animal."

"Mom, that's ridiculous!" burst in Ricki. Marcus had to silently agree with his daughter.

"Brigitte," he said in a gentle tone, "why don't you just say what you really think?"

Ricki's mother hesitated, but then she nodded. "All right, I will! I think that any animal that stays here costs money, and I hadn't planned on financing another horse with my household money. Anyway, I'm afraid of horses, whether they are big or small!"

"Well, at least that was honest," Marcus grinned. However, Ricki didn't feel like smiling.

"I'll give up my allowance," she offered spontaneously. "Maybe I could get a job delivering newspapers or –"

Carlotta, who had been listening attentively, interrupted Ricki,

"What if Salina belonged to me?" she asked, looking straight into Brigitte's eyes. "Would it be possible, then, to board her with you? I would take care of all the costs for the pony, including the vet costs that have been incurred up to now. That means you wouldn't have to do anything but keep her here in the stable, just like she's been for several weeks already."

Ricki held her breath and crossed her fingers tightly. She looked at her mother and tried, mentally, to signal to her; *Say YES, say YES, come on, say YES!*

"That's not a bad idea, Brigitte" responded Marcus.

Jake, who was just passing by and had heard what was being discussed, said instantly, "As far as I'm concerned, the little pony can stay here in the stable. She doesn't take much work. And she's an extremely sweet pony mare. But no one ever pays any attention to my opinion ..." And he kept walking. But he was hardly out of Brigitte's view when he winked at Ricki, almost making the girl laugh out loud.

Good old Jake, she thought. *If it weren't for you and Carlotta ...*

"Well, you can have another day to think about it, if you would like," the officer offered, but Carlotta shook her head firmly.

"No, no. I think we'll clear this up right away," she announced. "Now, Brigitte, once more, my question; Can I board Salina with you or do I have to find somewhere else for her?"

Brigitte looked at her in dismay. "The way you phrase the question, you've already decided to keep Salina, haven't you?"

Carlotta nodded. "That's right! You know, during my lifetime, I've seen too many horses who have been mishandled or just gotten rid of, just forgotten like an old hat. And I've seen animals shoved from one owner to another, so that at the end, they didn't know where they belonged. Animals have a right to love, too, and a home and a family. I think Salina has found her family in Diablo, Holli, Sharazan, Rashid, and especially in Chico. So, yes, it would make me really happy if you would decide to keep her, not just for the little pony's sake, but also for all of us who have already fallen in love with her."

Ricki had a huge lump in her throat as she listened to Carlotta's words. When the older woman was done, Ricki threw herself at her and gave her a big hug. She whispered, "Carlotta, you're an angel!"

Brigitte had also been moved by her friend's words. Now she looked from Ricki to Carlotta, somewhat undecided, and then cleared her throat.

"I think I've been outvoted," she replied and then her lips formed a little smile. "Well, all right, Carlotta. Your Salina can stay here."

"Yeah, Mom, thank you, thank you, thank you!" Ricki exploded, causing everyone present to jump with surprise. She immediately ran to the stable and came right back out leading Salina on a rope.

Ceremoniously, she handed over the little mare's rope to Carlotta. "Here, Carlotta! Salina wants to greet her new owner!" she called loudly, and then she hugged her parents as well.

"Thanks for letting Salina stay here," she kept saying, embarrassing Brigitte and Marcus in front of the police officer. He, however, just laughed and then stroked the pony underneath its thick mane.

"You're really lucky, you know that?" he said, laughing. Then, he turned to Carlotta.

"All I need from you is written confirmation that you are taking ownership of the animal."

Carlotta nodded and gave Ricki back the rope. "Go, take her back into her stall," she said, glancing at Ricki as the girl walked away. *She's getting more and more like me*, she realized before taking the prepared documents from the police officer. She had to fill in the date, her name, and her address on both copies, and then sign them.

"So, now we have one less problem. I hope you'll have a lot of fun with the new member of your family," commented Paul Stevenson. He tipped his hat and said goodbye to everyone.

They're all crazy, he thought, as he got in the car and reflected on Ricki's family. He could see it all clearly. *The old lady is as crazy as her granddaughter!* He had no idea how much the supposed grandmother, Carlotta, would have been pleased at the compliment.

*

Ricki and her friends were once again under way astride their horses, riding happily around Echo Lake.

"We haven't been here for ages," Lillian said.

"You're right! Hey, later we could go for a walk with Chico and Salina. I bet the two of them would love that," said Ricki.

Cathy commented, grinning, "Then you can count on having your brother tag along. You think you could stand that? He won't just let you take Chico from him. He'll want to lead him around himself."

"That doesn't matter. It's more important that the animals get to spend time outside than who gets to lead them. Anyway, Harry is usually easy to get along with when he's with Chico," said Ricki with a wink.

"How about a gallop?" asked Kevin, pointing to a trail that led out of the woods.

"Oh, yeah, great! What do you guys think? Want to go all the way to the Schultz farm?" suggested Lillian.

"Sure! That's one of the best trails around here for a gallop!" answered Ricki, beaming as she shortened Diablo's reins. "Everyone all set?" she asked. After each one of her friends had said okay, she gave free rein to her black horse.

She felt wonderful! Freed of any tension, she rid herself of all the problems of the past week with each galloping step that Diablo took. She found that her life – and all that went with it – was the greatest gift she had ever received. Yes, life was so wonderful, so magnificent, especially now that everything was cleared up with Kevin and Cathy, and even with Salina. Ricki was overjoyed.

Diablo seemed to gallop faster and faster, and Ricki had the feeling that her joy was being transmitted directly to her horse.

Gradually, the riders came closer and closer to the Schultz farm.

It's a shame, thought Ricki. *I could go on galloping like this forever!* Suddenly, she caught her breath and brought Diablo up short.

"Hey, are you out of your mind? You can't just put on the brakes like that! I almost rode right into you!" Lillian had just about been able to get Holli to ride past Diablo, slightly to the side.

Ricki pointed up ahead. "Do you see that? The slaughter-house transport is parked in front of the stable. I'd recognize that vehicle anywhere. It makes me sick to my stomach when I see it."

127

"What? Where? Are you sure?" Kevin had reined in Sharazan beside Diablo and was following Ricki's gaze. "Darn, you're right!"

"Which one of his horses does Schultz want to have picked up? I hope it's not old Jonah!" guessed Cathy. "He's soooo sweet!"

Ricki's expression hardened and her hands began to tremble.

She just couldn't understand how anyone could simply have his horse – who had served him faithfully its entire life – butchered just because it was too weak to work.

Turn around, she thought for a moment. She was sure that she wouldn't be able to stand watching the old horse as he got into the slaughterhouse van for his last ride.

Then she took a deep breath. "That just can't happen!" she said quietly but firmly. She looked at her friends. Without another word, the four teenagers galloped toward the stable, ready for action.

Ricki's inner joy was gone. There was no trace of the happiness that had filled her heart just moments before. Now sadness and fear gripped her and made it hard for her to breathe.

Jonah, she thought. *You can't die!* And she pushed Diablo to gallop even faster.

"Faster, boy, faster!" She urged him on and then had a hard time stopping him as she rode into the yard. Lillian, Cathy, and Kevin were following close behind.

Ricki was more out of breath than Diablo as she jumped down from the saddle.

Alarmed by the sound of horses' hooves on the brick

walkway, farmer Schultz came running out from the stalls, looking puzzled. Lillian was the first one he recognized.

"Oh, look who's here, Lillian! What are you doing here? Did your father send you?" he asked her warmly.

The girl shook her head. "No, Mr. Schultz, we ... we ..."

"Are you going to have one of your horses slaughtered?" asked Ricki, straightforward and upset. She stared at the farmer with enormous eyes.

"Oh, that's what this is about. I should have known," laughed the farmer. "I see that Ricki – the horse fanatic – is part of the crowd. You saw the van, didn't you?!"

The friends nodded.

"Well, yeah, you're right. Jonah is no longer useful for anything, and this is a working farm – not an old horses' resort home. Eating all day, and not doing any work ... I can't use a horse like that. When you consider what the insurance, the vet, and the blacksmith cost per year ... I'm sorry, but I'd rather buy a new, younger horse, before I end up paying more than Jonah's worth." He said it in a relaxed tone, as though he was chatting about the weather and not determining the death of an animal.

"And you can still laugh about it?" Ricki asked, outraged. "You want to have Jonah killed and you are in a great mood? That's ... that's just incredible."

Schultz looked at Ricki meaningfully. "Ricki, as a farmer, I just can't look at it that way. After all, I also breed cattle, and they end up being slaughtered. There's very little difference."

"That's just as cruel!" said the girl.

"But you enjoy eating your Sunday pot roast and barbecuing hamburgers, don't you? Where do you think the meat comes from? From my cattle!"

She stared at her friends helplessly. They had turned pale.

"Well, Mr. Schultz, my father is a farmer, too, but he sees it a bit differently. He would never think of slaughtering my Doc Holliday when he gets old," said Lillian seriously.

"You know what, Lillian, let's talk about that when the time comes! So, now ride back home and take care of your own horses!" responded the farmer brusquely. He stomped back into the stable.

"This is unbelievable!" Ricki stared at the transport van with frightened eyes. "He's as cold as a fish! I wouldn't have thought that of him!"

"And now?" asked Cathy. "Are we going to just ride back home, or – What *are* we going to do?"

Kevin's eyes were fixed on the open stable door. The *clip-clop* of Jonah's hooves could already be heard. "I think I'm going to be sick," said the boy. Ricki began to shake all over.

Lillian shook her head so fiercely that her hair flew in all directions. "I've known Jonah ever since I was a child. He was the first horse I ever rode," she said softly, wiping a tear from her eye.

"You're still here!" The farmer led his old gelding out of the stable and angrily glared at the four friends.

Jonah stood still. He glanced curiously at the other unknown horses, as behind him, Hank Ebersole, the driver of the transport, appeared.

"Did you order a going-away party or something?" Hank

teased, glancing at the young riders. They stared back at him, pale as ghosts.

"Don't fool around, Hank, get going. I have better things to do today than stand around in the yard with this old nag!"

Ebersole nodded and approached Ricki.

"Get out of the way!" he yelled at her.

While the driver let the loading ramp down with a bang, Ricki mounted her horse again. Her heart was beating wildly, and she sensed that Diablo was getting restless. He seemed to know what was happening here.

"Out of the way!" yelled Schultz at the four friends. He tried to lead Jonah to the ramp, but the gelding seemed to understand what was going happen to him. He stood stubbornly still, snorting excitedly as he glanced with fear at the transport.

Ricki wanted to scream, but she remained silent. *This isn't fair*, she kept thinking, as her eyes filled with tears. *Not Jonah! Not this dear old horse!*

"Now, come on, you stubborn old nag!" With all his strength, farmer Schultz pulled on the halter, but Jonah refused to budge. He stood firm, using his heavy weight against the farmer.

"Wait, I'll get a rope, and then we'll get him to move forward!" called Ebersole. He disappeared into the cab of the transport. "If this kindergarten class weren't standing here in the way, we'd be done by now!"

"That's right! Get out of here! You have no business being on my farm!"

Ebersole was back. He pulled a rope around the horse,

from the halter around the croup, and tied the end to the halter ring. Then he began to pull, while Schultz hit the horse hard on the croup.

"That's enough!" screamed Ricki suddenly. "Stop torturing this horse. That's mean ... that's really low!"

"She's starting to get on my nerves!" growled Schultz. He continued to push his horse from behind so that, slowly, Jonah was getting nearer to the loading ramp. The horse stared – frightened – into the dark insides of the vehicle.

Ricki couldn't stand it any longer. Bravely, she urged Diablo to stand right in front of the ramp, and she remained there with him.

"What's she doing?" whispered Cathy, scared, but Kevin just nodded and nudged Sharazan to move, too.

"She's doing exactly the right thing!" he replied, just as quietly. He placed Sharazan beside Ricki's black horse.

"That is just unbelievable!" yelled the farmer. He ran to Sharazan, grabbed the reins and pulled him aside, but, in the next instant, Lillian was standing at the same spot on Doc Holliday.

"You're making a midget rebellion here, but don't think for a minute that you're going to change anything! Miss Bates, get out of here! Fast!"

Schultz hit Holli on the croup so that the white horse jumped forward, but by then Cathy had also ridden up. The four horses made a living wall between the transport and Jonah.

Ebersole stood a few yards from the ramp with Jonah and scratched his head. He had never seen anything like this. Impatiently, he glanced at his watch. He should have been at the next customer's place by now, but from the look of things, this was going to take a long time.

Furious now, the farmer ran over to the stable and came back with a long whip. "Either you get out of here right now or I'm going to chase you and your horses away with a whip."

Ricki began to tremble even harder. She knew that Diablo had a fear of any kind of whip or switch.

"This isn't going to work," she whispered to Kevin, looking at him fearfully.

"He can't do that!" answered Kevin. He stared at the angry farmer, who was coming closer and closer, with the whip held high.

"If you hit them even once, you're going to be in terrible trouble with my father!" yelled Lillian suddenly. She looked at Schultz with fire in her eyes.

"Fine! I don't want to know what kind of trouble you're going to be in when your parents find out what you're doing here!"

"Please, Mr. Schultz, don't be mad, but Jonah ... he just can't be slaughtered." Ricki tried to calm him down, but the farmer wouldn't even listen.

"It's my horse, and I get to decide what happens to him! Enough of this!"

"But, Mr. Schultz, he's still healthy! Do you want someone to slaughter you when you get old?" yelled Lillian, She looked at Jonah, who now used all his strength to step backward, pulling Ebersole with him.

"That's enough, now! Ebersole, hold on to the horse! I have to make a phone call!" Schultz stomped off, and the kids looked at each other a little scared. They had no idea what was going to happen next.

*

The phone rang continuously at the Bates farm. Lillian's father hurried through the house, still wearing his stall boots.

"Yeah, Bates here," he answered grumpily. A flood of angry words rushed out at him.

He listened, silently, while his face grew more and more serious.

"It's okay, Arthur. I'm coming right over. Yeah, I understand ... No! Calm down, you know how the kids are. Yes! I'll be right there!" Dave Bates hung up and stared at Lillian's mother, who had just come in and was looking questioningly at her husband.

"Is something wrong?" she asked innocently before looking accusingly at her husband's filthy boots.

"Oh, yes!" he answered. "Lillian and her friends are at Schultz's farm and are blocking the transport of one of the horses to the slaughterhouse!"

"Oooh," responded Margaret Bates, exhaling loudly. "What now?"

"Now? First I'm going to the Sulais' to get Marcus. Then we have no choice but to drive out to Schultz's farm and try to make our daughters see reason while we calm down Arthur."

"Well, good luck with that! I wouldn't want to be in your shoes!" exclaimed Lillian's mother. A few minutes later, she watched her husband speed out of the driveway, tires screeching.

Chapter 9

"Ms. Mancini, Carlotta Mancini." Carlotta heard her name being called so she opened her door to see the familiar figure of the mail carrier.

"I have a registered letter for you, Ms. Mancini. I'll need your signature."

What's this all about? Carlotta wondered as she signed the receipt. *A registered letter? Must be important.*

She stood on her porch and opened the envelope.

Dear Ms. Mancini, the letter began. *It has come to my attention that you have assumed guardianship of the late Hiram Parker's pony, Salina. It will be in your interest to appear at the reading of Mr. Parker's last will and testament next Friday at one o'clock. Please advise if you are unable to attend.*

It was signed *C. L. Remington, Esq.*

What does this mean? Carlotta asked herself. *And what does Salina have to do with it?*

*

As she drove into the parking lot at the lawyer's office the following Friday, Carlotta again thought about the mysterious letter. *Maybe Mr. Parker had a distant relative who feels he has a right to the pony. That would be too bad*, she mused, *because I've really become attached to the little mare.*

She carefully closed her car door and locked it before limping on her crutches to the entrance of the old town hall, where Mr. Remington's office was located.

Mr. Parker's lawyer greeted Carlotta and then invited her to take a seat by his desk.

"You are probably surprised to find yourself all alone here in front of my desk," he began pleasantly. "However, Mr. Parker didn't have any relatives and his testament has a special clause in it."

"It's about Salina, after all," answered Carlotta and leaned forward with curiosity. "Why else would I be expected to come here?" She smiled back at him warmly.

"Let's continue with the opening of the testament ..." Solemnly C. L. Remington, Esq. put on his glasses and opened a sealed envelope.

"My last will ..." he began to read, slowly, enunciating clearly, while Carlotta listened with increasing astonishment.

*

"What was in the will?" asked Brigitte Sulai, looking expectantly at her friend.

Before answering, Carlotta took a large gulp of coffee from her cup. "Now I know where Ricki gets her sense of curiosity," she said, laughing. "You're even more curious than your daughter!"

"Well, I'm glad she didn't hear that," responded Brigitte.

"Okay. I'll leave out all the legal mumbo-jumbo and just tell you the important parts. Parker was a widower, as you know. He had no children, no relatives. The only thing he had in his life was little Salina, who now belongs to me."

"Yes, and?"

"But he did own some property: the farm, which he had recently renovated, and a huge tract of meadowland, which he had leased out to some of his neighbors. And this is where it gets interesting. Parker willed it all to the person who would take care of Salina after he was gone! What do you think about that?" Slowly and deliberately, Carlotta speared a piece of pound cake with her fork and transported it to her mouth.

Ricki's mother was incredulous and nearly dropped her coffee cup. "You mean you've inherited his farm and every-thing that goes with it because you took Salina?" she asked.

Carlotta nodded nonchalantly and turned her attention back to the cake. *That woman really knows how to bake,* she thought to herself.

"What are you planning to do with it?" Brigitte asked. "After all, you already have your own house. Are you going to sell the farm?"

Carlotta gazed into the distance and looked pensive. "I don't know yet, but I think ... I think I'm going to realize a very old dream of mine." Her face brightened.

"And that would be?"

Carlotta looked at Brigitte and laughed out loud. "If I tell

137

you, you'll probably think I'm crazy. Give me some time. I need to give all this a little more thought."

"You're not going to turn secretive on me, are you?" Brigitte teased. But Carlotta remained silent and kept her thoughts to herself.

Suddenly, they heard the sound of a car's horn honking in front of the house. Brigitte jumped up.

"What kind of an idiot −? Oh, it's Dave Bates!" She ran outside quickly, followed by Carlotta, who moved slowly on her crutches.

"Is Marcus here?" called Lillian's father.

"Right here!" Marcus appeared in the doorway almost at the same time as Brigitte.

"Come on, let's go! We have a problem!" said Dave. Without any explanation, he motioned Marcus into the passenger seat.

"What's up? Do you need me to help you with the birthing of a calf?" Ricki's father grinned. Then Dave explained the situation.

"They are crazy!" Marcus got into the car hurriedly.

"WAIT!" thundered Carlotta, who had overheard some of what had been said. "I'm coming with you!"

"Carlotta, don't get mixed up in this," Brigitte called after her, but Carlotta just shook her head vigorously.

"Well, then I'm coming, too!" Determined, Brigitte followed Carlotta toward the car.

"Marcus, get in the back. I need room for my legs!" commanded Carlotta as she eased herself into the passenger seat.

"Now we can go," she said, and slammed the car door shut.

*

Arthur Schultz stood in the doorway to his stable with a grimace on his face. He drummed his fingers against the wooden frame impatiently.

"So, what's going on here, Schultz? If you're not going to proceed, say so right now. I have other customers! Let's decide on another date when I can pick up the old nag."

"Oh, shut up, Ebersole! You're taking him today! Ah, finally!" Energetically, he leaped forward and ran into the center of the yard. He put his hands on his hips as Dave drove up.

Lillian and Ricki looked at each other with concern. The guy had actually called their parents!

"Uh-oh, here we go," whispered Lillian. She didn't feel quite as confident now that her father was here.

Ricki felt sick to her stomach. The only thing that gave her some courage was the sight of Carlotta, who had gotten out of the car with her parents and had given her an encouraging look.

In an instant, Carlotta understood everything. Her heart went out to these four courageous friends – acting without thinking of the consequences to themselves – who wanted to prevent this wonderful old horse from ending his days in the slaughterhouse.

"Did you teach your children to interfere in other people's business?" asked Schultz angrily, without even saying hello. "They are blocking my work here!"

"And mine, as well," Ebersole added grumpily. The four teens kept their horses firmly in place.

139

"Calm down, both of you. We're going to clear this up right away," said Dave.

"There's nothing to clear up! Get your rotten kids out of here!" Schultz yelled.

"My daughter is not a rotten kid! Do you understand?" Brigitte Sulai said angrily.

"Lillian, come here!" thundered Dave Bates. The fifteen-year-old jumped.

"Dad, please."

"I said, come here! Right now!" Lillian sensed that her father wouldn't tolerate any resistance. She gave Ricki a sad look before turning Holli. Lillian rode over to her father with her head bowed down.

"Would you please explain to me what this is all about? You don't have the right to interfere with other people's property. Mr. Schultz has the right to decide what happens to his horse!" he said, without looking at Jonah, who seemed to be listening to him with his ears straight up.

"But, Dad, Jonah is just old. Is that any reason to have him slaughtered?" Lillian tried to explain her viewpoint. Dave just shook his head vigorously.

"It's not up to you to decide," he repeated, although actually he agreed with his daughter.

"Kevin, Cathy, Ricki –" Dave Bates's voice became harsher. "You're just making things worse. Come on, now!"

Hesitantly, Cathy began to move away with Rashid. Finally Kevin gave in, too. Only Ricki and Diablo remained firmly in front of the ramp.

No! she rebelled internally. *This isn't going to happen! There must be a way to save Jonah.*

Marcus stared thoughtfully at his daughter. On one hand, he was furious that she had gotten involved – once again – in things that were none of her business. On the other hand, he was proud of her, that she had the courage to do something about things that were important to her.

I'm sure that if there had been room in our stable, she would have just taken off with Jonah, he thought, with a sidelong glance at his wife. Brigitte would have definitely freaked out in that case. Actually, Jonah really did look sweet, and Marcus had to admit that he was very impressive. Still, as much as it pained him, Marcus felt that he had to discipline his daughter.

Slowly, he walked over to Ricki while she stared at him. Her look hurt him deeply, because he understood how she felt.

"Ricki, it's no use. You have to get out of the way," he said softly to her. He was standing beside Diablo and looking up at her. "It's horrible, I know, but you can't save Jonah."

Marcus's gentle voice only made Ricki even more desperate. Tears ran down her cheeks while she looked at her father hopelessly.

"But, Dad, I ... I can't leave. I can't allow them to ... to kill Jonah just because he's old. You understand that, don't you?" Ricki's voice broke.

"Of course, darling. I understand you better than you realize, but try to understand Mr. Schultz's position. He needs animals that can work for him. This is a working farm, not an animal shelter. He uses his animals, and –"

"And that gives him the right to just have his animals slaughtered?" whispered Ricki weakly. "I'll never understand that."

"Come on, now," said Marcus and put his hand on her thigh. "Life doesn't always go the way we want it to."

"Will this stupid drama be over soon?" Arthur Schultz protested impatiently Marcus looked at his daughter pleadingly.

Slowly, Ricki let Diablo's reins slip out of her hands. She slid out of the saddle, while her father held on to the horse.

Tears ran down Ricki's face as she walked toward the huge workhorse. Her shoulders drooped dejectedly.

Ebersole stared at her and shook his head. How could anyone make such a fuss over an old nag? He just didn't understand it.

Incapable of saying anything, Ricki stood still directly in front of Jonah. The girl looked silently into Jonah's eyes for a long time.

I tried everything, you dear animal. I don't know what else I can do. People are so cruel, and I ... I'm ashamed. But that doesn't help you at all. Good luck, dear old Jonah. I'm sure that when ... when it's all over, you'll be better off than you were with Schultz.

Jonah held her gaze, and it seemed like he had understood her. He lowered his mighty head and breathed softly into Ricki's hair. Then he laid his heavy head on her shoulder.

Spontaneously, the girl wrapped her arms around his broad neck and pressed her face into his coat.

"So, Ebersole, you can finally bring that old horse over here." Schultz had gone over to the transport and gestured impatiently with his hands.

"All right, girl, get away from there. Now let's get down to business!" Ebersole jerked on Jonah's halter, while Ricki – her head bent and her heart heavy – stepped away.

I lost ... lost ... lost, she thought, unable to look at Jonah any longer. Frightened, she listened to the clapping of his hooves beating a pattern on the pavement. She had trouble breathing.

Jonah, it seemed, had resigned himself to his fate. Without stumbling or halting, he trotted slowly beside Ebersole.

"STOP!" Carlotta's voice cut through the silence and made Ricki turn around.

Schultz slapped his hand against the transport van. This just couldn't be happening!

"Keep going, Ebersole! Don't pay any attention to all this yapping. I'm paying you to load this nag and take him away!"

"And for my lost time," added Ebersole.

There were only ten feet between Jonah and his last journey, and suddenly he knew without a doubt what was going to happen. He raised his head and whinnied so shrilly that everyone there – except Schultz and Ebersole – was deeply touched. Once again, the animal turned his head to look accusingly at all the people who were standing around and not doing anything to prevent this.

"I said STOP!" Carlotta shouted again, lifting her crutches in a threatening gesture. "Mr. Schultz, how much money will you get from the slaughterhouse for this magnificent animal?" she asked, and limped over to the farmer, giving Ricki renewed hope. If Carlotta got involved, that might mean that –

"I don't know. Depends on the weight!" growled the farmer angrily. Ebersole stopped walking and looked back.

"How much does such an animal weigh?" Carlotta wanted to know.

Schultz shrugged his shoulders. He had reached a point where all he wanted was for this horse to disappear, and he didn't particularly care where to or how.

"I'll make you an offer," said Carlotta slowly. "I'll give you two hundred and fifty dollars for Jonah. In addition, I'll pay Mr. Ebersole's expenses for his trip here."

"Lady, you're crazy!" exclaimed Schultz. "As far as I'm concerned, you can take the beast with you! I'll be glad to have him out of my sight. But I get the two-fifty today, clear?"

"Of course," smiled Carlotta warmly. She gave Ricki the thumbs-up.

At first the girl couldn't even move. She stared at Carlotta in disbelief. Had she heard right? Was Jonah going to be saved after all?

"Yes, Ricki," said Carlotta, answering the girl's unspoken question. "Now get going! It's time to take Jonah home!"

Finally, the girl understood. "Yeaahhhhhh!!" she yelled victoriously, and this time it was tears of joy that filled her eyes.

She ran over to Jonah as fast as she could. She unsnapped the lunge from the halter and handed it to Ebersole, who was completely bewildered.

"Come, my dear old giant, let's get out of here before someone changes her mind," she called out. She led the unsuspecting Jonah over to the other horses, who greeted him with friendly whinnies.

Lillian, Cathy, and Kevin hugged each other, while Ricki beamed at Carlotta like a small child at Christmas.

"You are ... you're just ..." Ricki couldn't find the words to express her gratitude and relief.

"What are you trying to say?" Carlotta asked.

"You're the best thing that could have happened to Jonah!" exploded Ricki, as she fastened a calf rope from Dave Bates's trunk to his halter. Then she swung herself into Diablo's saddle and took the big draft horse on the lead to walk beside her.

"Take him to our farm first," said Dave as he grinned at Lillian's disbelieving face.

"What? Hey, people, what's going on? I have a feeling there's something I don't know. What's happening?" she asked.

Carlotta winked at Dave. She had quickly told him all about her plan and he had promised his help and support immediately.

"I'll tell you everything this evening!" promised Carlotta, with a suspenseful tone in her voice.

Brigitte began to have a vague idea ...

*

"I had the feeling back there that I was the one being led to the slaughter," Ricki tried to explain. She gazed lovingly at Jonah, who trotted happily beside Diablo.

"Jonah, are you aware that every step you take is a step

145

toward a new life?" laughed Lillian, as she bent down from the saddle and stroked the old draft horse across his mane.

"I think he knows that from now on he has nothing to fear," commented Kevin, before he guided Sharazan to the other side of Diablo.

"Hey, you," he said to Ricki. "I'm really proud of you! Who knows what would have happened if you hadn't been so determined!"

"You guys weren't so bad yourselves," she replied. Lillian waved her aside.

"Honor to those who deserve it," she said dramatically, causing all four friends to laugh out loud.

Only Cathy didn't laugh as loudly as the others. As happy as she was with the outcome, it had been Ricki – once again – who had shown courage and determination. It made Cathy a little sad that she couldn't be more like her friend and follow her feelings bravely and spontaneously.

*

Margaret was surprised to see her husband return from his mission in a good mood, and then quickly begin to fix up Holli's old stall.

"We're getting a temporary guest," he explained, grinning. Margaret laughed out loud.

"Don't tell me you talked Schultz into giving you this horse?" she asked, and Dave nodded.

"Guess whose idea it was?" he prompted.

"Hmm," she mused. "There are actually only three possibilities. Either it was Ricki or Lillian – which frankly I doubt – or it was Carlotta! She's the one I'd pick!"

"And you'd be right! Oh, by the way, there's some news! You won't believe what I'm going to tell you ..."

*

After the four youngsters had delivered their new friend safely to the Bates farm, and Jonah was happily chewing on a small mountain of hay, they rode back to the Sulais' stable.

"What luck. Our paddock is right between our two farms," said Ricki to Lillian. "We can let Jonah out every day and he won't be so alone!"

"Right! Oh, guys, I can't tell you how happy I am," raved Lillian. "We – No, Ricki and Carlotta – have saved my first riding horse, from when I was just a kid! Unbelievable! I could just hug all of you!"

"Don't force yourself," grinned Kevin. He waited in vain, however, because Lillian let out all her joy on Holli. She kept hugging him around the neck.

"It's too bad we don't have an extra stall here," complained Ricki, who would have liked to have all of the horses together.

"I'd like to know how Carlotta managed to get your father to take in Jonah," pondered Kevin, addressing Lillian. She just shrugged her shoulders.

"I don't care how she did it! The main thing is that Jonah is still alive!"

"Exactly!" Ricki had just finished cleaning Diablo's hooves and now she was peering over the top of the stall at

Cathy and Rashid. "I'm anxious to hear what Carlotta has to tell us."

Cathy nodded. "So am I, but she can be very secretive."

"Hey, are you finished yet? Your Rashid is as shiny as a new penny," Lillian announced.

Cathy rolled her eyes. "It takes time to create true beauty," she answered, before leaving the dun-colored horse in his stall.

"Carlotta's here!" reported Kevin with a glance out the window.

"What? Here already? Let's go, everybody. I am so curious, I can't wait to hear what she has to say."

Quickly, the kids put away their grooming kits. They were so anxious to listen to Carlotta's plan that they almost knocked down Jake on their way out of the stable.

"Hey, slow down," he was just able to get out of the way before Ricki slid to a stop right in front of him.

"Oh, Jake, sorry. Have you already heard, that –?"

"Yes! You guys sure do make a lot of noise, but – seriously – it's great what you did to save that horse!" said the elderly stable man, as he followed the youngsters into the Sulais' house. "What are we going to discuss that's so important?" he asked Ricki, but before the girl could answer him, they heard Brigitte's voice.

"We're in here ... in the kitchen!" she called.

"Well, then, let's follow my mother's voice," grinned Ricki as she pushed open the door to the kitchen.

Carlotta, Marcus, and Harry were already seated around the kitchen table, while Brigitte was making sandwiches.

"I hope you're hungry, otherwise we'll be eating leftover sandwiches for a week," Ricki's mother laughed.

Lillian reassured her: "Don't worry, Mrs. Sulai. Kevin's here too, and by the time he leaves, you'll be lucky to have anything left in the refrigerator."

Kevin grinned. He was already engrossed in deciding which sandwich on the plate he was going eat first.

"So, Brigitte, sit down, please." Carlotta pointed to the only vacant chair.

"Tell us, please, Carlotta, what's your plan? We're all going to burst if you don't tell us soon!" urged Ricki.

"Now I can start," said Carlotta, looking from one to the other with a giant smile on her face. "For anyone who doesn't already know, today I inherited Hiram Parker's farm, and –"

"What?" Ricki interrupted. "How did he decide on you?"

"He didn't pick me. He just willed his property to whomever would take care of Salina after his death!" explained Carlotta for the second time that day. "I've told you that so you can understand what I'm going to tell you now."

"Ever since I was a young girl, I've had a dream," began Carlotta, her eyes becoming soft. "I've always imagined how wonderful it would be to provide a home and shelter for needy, aging animals – mainly horses – that are simply disposed of by their owners –"

"Like Jonah," added Ricki. Kevin poked her on the leg.

"Let Carlotta finish her story," Kevin insisted.

"Okay, okay," she said softly, as Carlotta continued.

"There have been many times during my life when I've tried to realize that dream, but something always happened to prevent me: my career with the circus, personal problems,

149

my accident, any number of circumstances. So at some point I just resigned myself to the idea that when the time was right, I would know it." Carlotta paused and looked at each of them solemnly before continuing.

"When Mr. Parker's will was read today, and I actually faced the possibility of realizing my dream, I began to worry that I couldn't begin such a project in my old age. But today, when I was at the Schultz farm and I saw you all so committed to saving that old horse from the slaughterhouse, I dismissed my doubts. You all showed me that when it comes to helping animals, it doesn't matter how old or young you are. And so I've decided to make my childhood dream a reality. I will open a home for retired, old horses, and Jonah will be the first guest to spend the rest of his life happily on my farm. That's the reason, Lillian, that your wonderful father agreed so quickly to take Jonah until the home can be opened. And that will happen sooner than you think. I promise you!"

I knew it, thought Brigitte and nodded to Carlotta. The others just sat there completely overwhelmed by her words.

Suddenly, Ricki began to applaud enthusiastically. Kevin joined in, then Lillian, Cathy, and finally all those present gave the former-circus-rider-turned-philanthropist the best round of applause she'd ever received.

"I've said this once today, but it's worth repeating," said Ricki in a solemn voice: "Carlotta, you are a real-life angel ... a guardian angel for horses!"